LILA SAYS

'What an extraordinary book *Lila Says* is – and not
simply because the identity of its author remains a
mystery.

'This is the passionately written story of a nineteen-
year-old unemployed Arab living on one of the "no-
go" housing estates outside Paris, who becomes
obsessed with the beautiful, seductive, blonde Lila.
Their relationship is immediately gripping, but what
I also took away from the book were the details of a
foreign world that is at once fascinating and hopeless.

'The book is deeply erotic, shocking even . . . but
it is first and foremost a beautifully written love story
and, I believe, a classic. I started reading *Lila Says*
one rainy morning in a French café. Unable to stop,
I ordered coffee after coffee until I̶ ̶ ̶ ̶ ̶ ̶ ̶ ̶ ̶ ̶ ̶
dramatic, haunting end.'

D1354998

LILA SAYS

translated by David Watson

FOURTH ESTATE • *London*

This paperback edition published in 1998

First published in Great Britain in 1997 by
Fourth Estate Limited
6 Salem Road
London W2 4BU

Copyright © Plon, 1996
English translation © David Watson, 1997

3 5 7 9 10 8 6 4

The right of David Watson to be identified as the translator of
this work has been asserted by him in accordance with the
Copyright, Designs and Patents Act 1988.

A catalogue record for this book is available from the British
Library.

ISBN 1–85702–565–2

Typeset by Avon Dataset Ltd, Bidford on Avon B50 4JH
Printed in Great Britain by Clays Ltd, St Ives plc,
Bungay, Suffolk

LILA SAYS

S he stops, she starts off saying:

'You see I've got the face of an angel, everyone tells me that. See my eyes, they're clear and blue, you'd give them all you've got in the world.

'See my hair, it's so blonde, my aunt says it's as if silkworms shat gold just for me.'

I don't know why she's talking to me like this. Then she says:

'My skin, my aunt says my skin is Saint Lawrence's paradise. They burned Saint Lawrence on a grill, so my aunt says he'd have deserved to live on skin like mine for the rest of eternity. See my hands, they're fine, white and soft, when I put them together then God will agree to anything.'

She stops for a moment, she lowers her head, then she raises it and says:

'My voice, I talk to you, you know it. It's like a christening bell, my aunt says, like the wind in a meadow in May – she talks like that, my aunt, and

1

she's as ugly as an old boot. Worst thing is she doesn't realise. Do you know her?'

I tell her I don't.

'She doesn't realise so she does herself up like a fairground ride. Three hours every morning in front of the mirror with her brushes and then she stays at home.'

Actually, I do know her aunt, I saw her one day at her broken window on the sixth floor cursing everything under the sun.

Then she says: see my arms, see my legs, they're like this and that, I forget what her aunt said, oh yeah, her legs would make a lovely necklace for Saint Christopher, her feet could walk on water. Her feet wouldn't sink, because it's sins that weigh you down, that's why you drown.

That's how she sees the world, her aunt.

We're both standing there near the sand pit, the children have all gone home. You can hear all the tellies on the same channel, the game show's starting – round here everyone dreams that the arrow of the wheel of fortune will point to them – and also the Arabic radio stations which I can hardly understand. You can see that the trees don't move, like they were made of concrete painted dark. And then the guy who works as a supervisor at the Mammouth supermarket comes home on his second-hand moped, you feel like calling the fire brigade it's belching out so much black smoke, and every evening, so that no one can nick it, he carries it up the stairs to the third floor, he's like a mountain biker of the tower blocks.

Then just like that she says:

'Want to see my pussy?'

I don't say yes or no, sort of as if I didn't hear. There's no doubt about what she said, but I wait a bit. I just see how things develop. I'm not the sort to jump out of the first open window even if the sun is shining.

So she goes on about her pussy:

'You know, my aunt wants to see it every morning and every evening. She sits in front of it and looks at it for ages and it really pisses me off. And I get cold. She pats her hands together as she talks. It's the gateway to the happy valley where the sun always shines. She tells me things, you don't know where she gets them from, like how there's this wonderful genie locked up in there who'll burst out one day, if he ever gets hold of Ali Baba's tin-opener.'

And so on and so on. She makes up poems about her pussy all day long, her aunt. It's a little gem of ripped silk, with its little sleeping tongue, the swelling, tucked-in lips that will never get crumpled. Not like her worn-out old mound (says Lila). It's so blonde it could be a lantern when you've lost your way . . . With your eyes closed you could follow it by the smell alone up to the fount of eternal youth. It's a prayer, a balm, a treasure island, the choicest delicacy of Jesus Christ.

This is the second time she's gone on at me about her pussy. The first time it was just a question like that then nothing, as if she forgot about it straight away. That's why I'm waiting to see how things develop. See if she really has got something to boast about.

And don't be surprised (anybody out there reading this) that even though I live almost directly opposite the Islamic Centre, I keep going on all the time about Saint Lawrence and the like. It's because her aunt is a Christian, and so is Lila no doubt. I don't know how come she turns out to be a Christian, maybe it's just to be different, or it's from her family. They say her aunt makes the sign of the cross when she greets the postman. Her mouth is always stuffed with holiness, she could choke on it. She has heaven and the Blessed Virgin all over the place, and blessed be the name of the Angel Gabriel, and all the others, except Saint Paul, she can't stand him, he's way too macho, it was a big mistake to make him a saint, she says.

It's me writing all this but it's not me that's going on about religion, it's Lila's aunt. I don't have much to do with God myself, seeing as how he has forgotten me along the way. I don't know him, or the saints either. My dad used to say when he was still at home that sometimes you look around and there's nothing but dust.

And how come the girl is blonde? The Norwegians certainly don't come here for their holidays. I bet Lila is the only natural blonde around here. So blonde she looks like a stain. My dad used to say that once you used to see women dyed blonde by the Devil, but now Islam has put a stop to all that. You have to respect God's work, if he made you ugly and lame he has his reasons.

So they dye one lock of hair and hide it under a scarf, some of them even do their pubes, just to feel they're rebelling somehow.

She says again:

'Don't you want to see my pussy?'

'How much?' I ask.

'Whatever you like.'

'I haven't got anything.'

'I know you haven't got anything,' she says. 'I wasn't talking about cash. I didn't say it because I wanted you to pay for it. Of course, I know you haven't got anything. No one round here has anything. If I wanted to make money out of it I'd go somewhere else.'

'Why did you say it, then?'

'Just to give you a treat. I thought you might like it.'

When she talks, I'm not kidding, it's like the air tingles. I don't know how to explain it, something you can't see, only feel. Her voice makes everything move, yet she doesn't speak very loudly. Even the trees that seem like they're made out of concrete are touched when she talks. According to her aunt, who's told the postman about it, it's the voice of purity, it's the voice that sings in the streams and launches a thousand ships.

I've got notes all over the place and now I'm trying to put them in order. I realise I've started this notebook back to front, so the red line's on the right.[1] But it's too late to start again. I write very slowly,

---

[1] Indeed, the first notebook of the manuscript is written back to front, so the margin is on the right.

trying not to make any mistakes. I hurry but I don't know if I'll ever reach the end. It's amazing how long it takes, I had no idea. I've never even read a book right through, so to write one . . .

So, getting back to her blondeness and how she looks like a stain, and where she could have come from, with her colouring and her corn-coloured angel's hair, even her aunt, who is dark turning to grey, with a hint of purple, seems to think that it comes from a long way back. Sometimes it goes back forty or fifty generations, then up it pops all of a sudden, and there's a blonde in a dark family. Even the experts don't know why; it's like seeing a McLaren one morning in the car park of Block H.

Then she says:

'Don't you want me to show it to you?'

'Why do you want to show it to me?'

'I told you. Because I feel like it this evening.'

With that voice like a wire humming in the air.

'But not other evenings?'

'Not necessarily.'

'Why not?'

' 'Cos you're not the only one.'

'So you've shown it to others?'

But she doesn't reply, she starts to sing a Vanessa

Paradis song and the words seem to come out without her moving her lips, just a wind with notes.

So obviously, seeing as we're alone, and it could be now or never, I say yes, actually I do want to see it.

'Do you want a long look or a short look?'

I'm not sure what she means. I'm slow on the uptake sometimes.

'Long look or short look?' she repeats.

'What's the difference?'

'Short look I lift my skirt, just a quick flash to show I've got nothing on underneath. Long look is on the slide.'

'The slide's not that long,' I say.

'Shit!' she says. 'You can be a right pain! It's free, you didn't even have to ask and you're still complaining. Now's your chance since I want to do it with you, otherwise that's it! I'll leave you there with your tongue hanging out for ever, I'm warning you! Don't come crying that others have seen it and not you!'

Even when she gets cross her voice doesn't hurt you. It's more like a kiss of anger, or like a puppy's tongue finding out how hard life is. Besides, everyone round here is foul-mouthed even when they just saying hello, how are you. Nothing is ever OK, everything's crap; life is made up of tiny, useless bits, in the morning you don't even have any plans for the evening, no plans that will come to anything, when you wake up you just think about going back to sleep, you want the night to come quickly, otherwise you're hanging around, nothing to do, no cash, just nothing, nothing.

So the chance to see her pussy, it's like winning the jackpot, or like an ocean voyage. Something like that. My heart has been enlightened, it has become a sun.

'The slide,' I say.

I know some other girls who have done it, but they were smaller. It's a kids' thing really. Later, when they grow up, they don't dare any more. A Muslim brother might come by with his black nails.

I'm nineteen. She's sixteen and a bit, I think. I don't know exactly.

It's already the evening and there's nobody around any more. Bakary, Ali, Little Maurice and Big Jo are down at La Courneuve doing some business. I heard them say there was a load of electric blankets to be had. I don't do stuff like that – they have a go at me sometimes, but I still don't go.

No wind, not a breath. The lights are on in the windows, but outside it's still light enough to see. It's early June. It hasn't rained for at least two months. You think you're breathing air, but it's dust, even at night.

She climbs to the top of the slide up the wooden ladder and I stay standing in the sand pit, though I move over a bit so I'm facing the slide.

She sits down right at the top without a word. She smiles at me. All this just for me. She lifts her dress, which is a sort of pale blue (I forgot to mention that she always wears a dress, which also makes her different), but she's still got her legs out straight and pressed together and her feet pointing up. Then she closes her eyes and launches off, and at the same time, her party trick, she opens her legs in a wide V and I hold my breath – she really has got nothing on underneath, I see her pussy giving me a quick look as it sweeps down into the bend, blonde and curly, I swear to God, it's like the tip of one of those paper planes kids make in class, except it's less well defined, it doesn't start or end anywhere, but it's golden, it's the triangle in the golden mist, hurtling towards me through the bend, I see nothing but that, the star down below, it lasts, what? long enough to say fucking hell fucking fucking fucking hell then it all crashlands in the sand. It's going to need a good dusting down after that. If only I could turn myself into a little brush with soft bristles. Can anybody hear me? Come to me, great magician, please turn me into a brush.

But it's not all over. She gets up patting down the light blue fabric, her eyes lowered, concentrating carefully she comes towards me on those legs that could dance on clouds, then when she gets up close she stops, she lifts her head and looks at me, and says:

'Did you get a good look?'

'No,' I say.

'Why not?'

'It was too quick.'

'The slide's like that.' she says to me, her eyes transparent. 'It's not my fault. I didn't go quick on purpose. You can't go slower, that's how it is, unless I had a rope holding me back. Anyway, you know,' she says, coming a little closer, 'it's better when it's quick.'

I ask her why, she says:

'It's not something you should look at for too long.'

I'm standing there not knowing what to say. There are times like this when she leaves me speechless. My mouth is full of the earth of the Sahel – I don't know the Sahel, but I've heard people talk about it.

So I don't say anything. She gives me a moment or two, her little face white and innocent – she could drag anything out of you, I swear, her little, fine, pure head you wouldn't dare touch a hair, a face from heaven, lily white, the face of a young saint, that's how I imagine her.

So at that moment she says:

'Are you looking at my face?'

I tell her I am.

'Do you like it?'

I tell her I do.

'Everyone likes it,' she says, 'but have you had a good look?'

'I think so,' I tell her. Though it is starting to get dark.

'Have you seen my mouth?' she says (this was yesterday).

I tell her I have, she repeats:

'No, look at my mouth for a bit. Have you seen my mouth? Have you had a good look? Have you noticed how tiny it is?'

I tell her yes, I've noticed.

'Amazing, isn't it?' she says, totally serious, her big eyes open wide, see-through blue.

'What's amazing?'

'That such a small mouth,' she says, 'could swallow a big cock.'

Those were her exact words, I'm not making it up.

I look at her and say nothing. I think at that precise moment I have stopped breathing. But I say nothing. I'm not sure I could even speak.

'I couldn't believe it,' she explains, without moving an inch. 'The other day I found myself looking in a mirror while I was sucking a really nice one. You wouldn't have recognised my mouth. Wide open like a sack. Like a snake swallowing a lamb. And this cock was all the way in, right down to his balls, don't know where I found room, although it made a bump at the side, in my cheek. Your lips are elastic, when you see it you can't believe it. More than your arse even. They stretch, if you see what I mean, they go out of shape, they get so wide it's frightening. I like to watch myself sucking. I like doing it and at the same time I'm on show, a free show at that. Not to mention the feeling, especially when he goes off and it's all warm, running down my cheeks and I get some on the tip of my tongue. But most of all, when I do it, you know what gives me the most pleasure? It's the thought that a little angel is getting off.'

I hardly know her, just to say hello to really. Here in the sand pit is the first time she's spoken to me, in that singing voice you'd walk through thorns for, that voice that is never guilty, which does bad but never on purpose, a voice that makes you believe in miracles, that announces the departure of flights that will never return in leather-bound airports.

I stand there shaking.

She probably notices.

'What's your name?' she asks.

'Chimo.'

'Mine's Lila, like the flower without the *c* on the end. Where does it come from, Chimo?'

'I don't know.'

Now she climbs out of the sand pit, she shakes out her white dancer's shoes and she balances on the wooden side, leans forward, leans back, once she nearly loses her balance and grabs hold of my arm, smiling.

I'm not there any more, I don't know where I am but I'm not there. Which shows that she's not looking at me any more. She is looking distractedly round at Block F, then Block C, then the tower. It's getting even darker, three or four hundred windows are lit up around us, but her hair shines strongest of all.

She turns her back to me, she shows me her profile once without turning her head my way at all. I feel completely gormless, I would like the night to bare its teeth and swallow me. Her profile stands out sharply against what is left of the light. I don't have the words for it. Someone like her you can't call a babe, a chick, a tart, a bit of skirt. Those words don't suit her, they're not for her, you can't even call her a girl. She is unique, she needs a word all of her own.

Softly she goes now, balancing on top of the wooden plank, her arms stretched out on each side, pointing her fingers to the ground. It's a while now since she last looked at me. I don't know which of us really exists.

She goes and I stay.

She doesn't say anything more to me this time.

At night I often pretend to sleep, then I get up and I write. I go into the kitchen to the little folding table where it's quiet and there's water to drink. Sometimes during the day as well, when I can't resist it, I take my notebooks, I tell the others I'm going to the agency or the surgery, once I say I'm off, I've had enough, don't come after me, and I go to a little place only I know about, a building site they closed down because of corruption. There's this half house still standing from the time when there were still houses with chimneys and roofs – just the front and the corner of a dining room they haven't yet reduced to rubble, with shreds of peeling wallpaper still on it, cherries or plums, and loads of copper and glass among the debris and a broken old door – it makes you think about the meals they had in there and the parties – and grass, surprisingly tall, you wonder how it manages to grow – it's just like us, grass among the ruins my friends – and in there

I've built myself a writing desk out of stacked-up lumps of plaster then some old stones and another pile to sit on. I call it my office, I go there with my notebooks and pens except when it's raining. And except at night, I don't have a light.

They are squared notebooks, I stole them from the market.

I don't know how to write but I've got the taste for it, the desire.

At school the others do nothing but chat, yawn, crack their fingers, fart like they're having a contest, scrawl obscenities all over the place sometimes in shit with their hands. Mouloud once took out a gun in class, his brother's. Or else they shout insults at the teachers, some of them would leave in tears – I can still see my French teacher standing red-eyed at the bus stop in the rain – the ones with cars they punctured their tyres or broke their windows, and they always pinched the fire-extinguisher from the school corridor, which is not an easy thing to sell. I tell myself maybe it was stupid not to make the most of school, to just think about raving, doing drugs and a spot of breaking and entering, a bit of money to be had, everything in the short term. The end result is when you leave it's like you're old already and you know nothing, absolutely nothing, and more often than not the cops know who you are – you find yourself footloose and filthy in a world of concrete, out of work, you're not such a big mouth now, and why should anyone offer you work since you know nothing. Come on, off to jail with you.

My dad used to say that walls were the notebooks of fools.

Mind you, I was just the same myself, I knew it all and I didn't give a damn, well pissed off at being stuck at a desk having to listen to stupid stories, like how the French Revolution changed the world, which makes you wonder what sort of god awful state we were in before, and how light is made up of both waves and particles at the same time, I remember no one could explain that to me, but that's not what makes the figs ripe in any case – all these things which are no use to anybody except to talk about, and you can't even understand them because you're not equipped for that, and no one ever explained it to your dad.

But I was really into French classes and essays, I never missed any, I always wrote longer ones than everyone else, my pen moved across the page like a trail of flies. I never finished on time, and even though the teacher with the red eyes used to yell at me like Hitler because of my handwriting, which wasn't as bad as the others', by the way, and my aversion for negatives as she put it, with deep sighs like a big ball punctured by a nail, even so she often gave me good marks and a couple of times I was top. One day she waited behind to speak to me after the lesson, she started saying this and that, that I always surprised her with the way I wrote and maybe one day I should do some – some what I'll never know because at that moment my mates all burst in shouting teacher's pet, crawler, arse-licker, you sleeping with her or what, and so she left me standing there and she never spoke to me again face to face.

I think it's a shame really, because I stayed keen as I got older, though I do it in secret now, on my own. I'm aware my pen moves more slowly, that I'm not too hot on vocabulary and grammar. It's hard even finding the ideas – at school at least the teacher gave you the subject, now you have to find everything yourself. It's like hard labour stringing the words together, in my kitchen or my ruins, and it really takes something to finish it. I tell myself I'm going to write such and such, I set off like I'm chasing a thief, but I lose it, so I set off on something else, that slips out of my head, and that's how it goes. I feel too much on my own to write, especially when it won't come out on paper, it's there somewhere, it's all over my body, maybe somewhere else too – I don't know where exactly, it's impossible to locate, like an itch you want to scratch to relieve it, but no, it's moved off somewhere else, you run and run. I once saw a clown on telly who was trying to catch a piece of soap, the soap kept leaping out of his hands like a frog, and it's the same with me, my doors are wide open all the time, the breeze blows in to my heart. These feelings that make me quiver like the sun in winter, I don't know exactly what they are, they seem as beautiful as the sky, but when I try to write them down they come out like lukewarm water.

That's where Lila is such a blessing – I'm sounding like her aunt – she's the great gift from a generous heaven, I could tell with the story about the slide how easily it all came out, I'm there, I listen, I write, it even gets easier the more I do, and the writing gets less shaky. No more need to rack my brains trying to think of something to say, I'm a tape recorder now, I record Lila talking.

One day I was in my den, this was before Lila, when this little kid of about seven or eight turns up, she's got plaits, thick glasses on her nose and an empty cage in her hand, she comes in and sees me there and straight off she tells me she's sad, that she's lost her hamster Léon and she's been looking for him everywhere, she's afraid the dogs will gobble him up, or the rats, which are so nasty round here, and have I seen him prowling around in the rubble. I tell her I haven't, but if I do of course I'll catch him. She's about to go when she looks at me through her thick lenses and asks in a curious way what I'm doing there on my pile of plaster. I tell her I'm doing nothing, that I'm writing. So she purses her lips and says contemptuously (she's white): 'How can you write in here, it's so dirty?' And she goes off with a grimace, forgetting about Léon, not even interested in what I'm writing.

All right, I'm dirty, but I don't know what that means really, since this whole estate stinks of piss, and worse, people just throw their rubbish down the stairs or out the window, that's how much affection they have for the place, sheer contempt. You don't walk under the towers in case you get an old fridge landing on your head, or dirty water or shit, since the sinks are often blocked, and the bogs – it's incredible how quickly things fall apart round here, the lifts most of all, they're always fucked, so the repair men get fed up with it, so after a while they stop coming, so the old people have to struggle on the stairs with their shopping – that's another reason why they don't bring their rubbish down.

Same with the things they throw away, no one bothers to collect them any more, except once every three months or so a gang of Pakistanis and Afghans turns up with hammers, screwdrivers, the odd blow-torch, they come to salvage what they can – bolts, wires, bits of wood, even empty pen cases, which they use to make radios with and other things apparently. They can find a use for anything, they're pillagers, it's a laugh watching them, they talk very fast in their own language, they've got this van that shakes like it's dead scared. The stuff they leave behind just rusts and rots where it lies, it's eaten by fleas and lice, all the vermin of the non-human kind. Jo's dad says he's even seen seagulls come up from Le Havre some days when the wind's in the right direction to help with the tidying up.

I'm stopping there for today, I haven't seen Léon, I don't know what else to say.

22

I'm coming out of Mammouth with two white carrier bags – I'm doing the shopping for my mother, it's Tuesday – when I hear Lila's voice calling me: hi there! she's coming out too through another door, carrying a bag. She undoes the lock on her bike, a man's bike I notice, and she says:

'You going home?'

I tell her that I am.

'How are you getting there?'

'On a horse,' I say with a straight face.

She knows I'm on foot, since I haven't got anything else.

'If you do the pedalling,' she says, offering me the bike, 'I'll sit on the crossbar and we can go back together.'

'What about the bags?'

'We can put one on the rack and hang the other two from the handlebars. We'll manage. So are you on for it?'

Obviously I'm interested. The estate is over a mile away, I've had enough opportunities to measure the distance, in the sun and in the rain. And why kid myself, I get a thrill out of being with her.

We do what she suggested with the carrier bags, one on each handlebar for balance, the other one well strapped on the back. I settle myself on the saddle and she hops up and sits across the crossbar, she says push, let's go. I push off, it wobbles all over the place at the start, Lila cries oh, I'm scared, I'm scared, but she's laughing at the same time, I press as hard as I can, come on Chimo she says, we're zigzagging so much around the car park this old dear says you're bonkers, then I find my rhythm and we're off along the main road, then down the Avenue Émile-Zola.

She hangs on to the frame with both hands, her hair is right in front of my face, I've never been this close. It's finer than words can say, like the golden grass in fairy tales, I'm singing these words quietly to myself, she has a cloud of gold over her head. When I breathe it ruffles, then falls back in a different shape. I'm watching the road and the traffic through this fabulous foam, and every now and again, lower down, when she shifts position slightly or when we go round a bend, I see the hollow of her shoulders and the

24

neckline of her dress, where there are two eggs nestling quite close together, trembling a little but never breaking, you can't see what's holding them there, they're as beautiful as beauty itself, so soft you can tell by looking, if I was an insect in between those two I'd die happy.

She must be aware of what she's showing me, yes, obviously she knows. I don't know how she knows, it's a female thing, but she does know – a lot of girls flaunt it in a really tacky way, with their dresses barely covering their arses and knee-high boots, then they're surprised when they get raped down in the cellars.

Sometimes your thoughts talk to each other, it's weird. Eggs make me think about her thighs down below, her thighs make me think of her pussy, and at that moment, as if she's reading my thoughts, she asks:

'Do you remember when I showed it to you?'

'What?'

'You know what I'm talking about. You remember on the slide?'

'Yeah.'

She shows me her profile and projects her words into the street.

'Do you think about it sometimes?'

'Yes, I think about it,' I say.

'Do you think about it a lot?'

'It depends.'

'Once a day, or more?'

'About once a day.'

This time she puts her head right back so she's looking me straight in the eyes, her head is in contact with my right arm, I'm seeing her almost back to front, and she says:

'Would you like to see it again? What do you say?'

'Oh . . .' I say.

'Oh what?'

'If you like.'

'It's not for me to say,' she says. 'If I'm offering it to you it means I'm willing. So do you want to see it again?'

'Yes.'

'When?'

'I don't know when.'

'Now, here?'

I'm not sure what she means, if she's thinking about doing it on the bike or what. I don't say anything.

She says:

'At this precise moment it's lying right over the crossbar.'

I wish she'd stop there, not say any more, because I'm a bit shy, I feel embarrassed even out in the middle of the street, I'm afraid she's going to say some more, so I ask her:

'Whose bike is it?'

'A friend's,' she replies. 'He lent it to me.'

'What friend?'

But she doesn't seem to hear, she continues, turning her head around as she speaks:

'When I sat down I made sure my clit was right on the bar, every little jolt gives me a nice feeling, just think, it's like the street is touching me (then she says a couple of words I don't catch). Men don't understand, the movements of nature. It's different for women, we follow the cycles of the moon, our periods and everything, we're like little planets.'

With every bump she goes hmm, hmm, with her eyes closed.

I try to keep on the flat bits because she's really winding me up.

'And then there's this big stiff thing underneath me.'

I keep my mouth shut on purpose. After all, I don't know her, it's only the second time we've met just the two of us.

And then:

'I can show you it, you know. You don't even need to stop. Don't you believe me?'

I don't reply.

'Get some speed up,' she says, 'then stop pedalling, you'll see.'

I do as she says, I pick up speed, it's downhill in this direction on the Avenue Émile-Zola, then I stop pedalling. She places a foot on one of mine, holds on to the frame with one hand, like a circus acrobat – the bike's leaning over but I hold it steady, keep it rolling – she pushes herself up off my foot, turns up her dress with her other hand and says:

'Look.'

What else can I do but look, I'd have to be a monkey not to, and I see it, see it again right down below. If it was a landscape it would be like a little summer wood disappearing at the foot of a hill, or a handful of blonde leaves caught in the hollow of a stream – I'm trying to work out how to put it, the only streams I've seen have been on the telly, round here they've buried them underground. It's something you can't see but you know it's there, the tuft, the bush, all still, so you'd never guess there's this wide red slit lower down which is a bit scary, which she showed me on the slide, and which some other girls have given me a quick look at three or four times before, but never fair like this. From above it looks like a few innocent hairs, nothing to worry about, no precipice, no danger.

Then she lets go of her dress and she says:

'Was it good like that too?'

'Yeah,' I say, 'not bad.'

'Did you like the slide better?'

'It's not the same.'

'I can show you something else,' she says.

'What?'

'Let me do the pedalling, you'll see. Other way.'

Since I don't know what she means, she tells me to keep a hold of the bike, then she swings round smoothly on the crossbar, dangles her right leg over the right-hand side, still gripping the frame tight. I let go of the pedals, she takes them over, pushes hard to get the bike moving again, right there in front of me, she's doing all the work, breathing hard, and I hear her say between breaths:

'Lift my dress up a bit and have a look.'

I always hesitate when she suggests something, but I know I'm going to do it anyway, so I lift up the dress with one hand, holding on to the saddle with the other, and I see something I've never seen, a young girl's bum at work, thighs pumping away, her pussy in the middle pulling one way then the other, but still staying more or less closed, and protected, just above, the arsehole which is dancing around too of course, so much it even lets off a little fart, which makes Lila laugh, even though she is working hard, and after that she says:

'Lean back, you'll see better.'

I already know she's right, and indeed if I lean my body back and put my legs out straight for balance I can see in the shadow of the dress the whole pedalling kaboosh, thighs and everything, with those closed lips, hanging down a little, thicker than you would have thought seeing them from the front, there they are in the middle, framing the entrance to the mystery, the colour of bright raspberry.

I'm wondering whether the people passing by are noticing what we're doing – I'm sure some of them must be having a good ogle, but Lila doesn't care and neither do I, it's as if the avenue was the desert just before heaven, and we are the only two people, her showing, me looking.

'OK?' she asks. 'Had a good look?'

I don't say anything, I'm still looking too hard. I've never seen this before and there's a fair chance I'll never see it again. That's what I say to myself when something happens to me, which isn't very often. So I see it: the little machine that makes the world go round.

'I'm tired, take over the pedals.'

We change over, she swings her right leg back over to the left side, that's the end of the vision. She settles herself back in her former position on the frame, catches her breath, coughs a bit, moans oh and ah, then says:

'Did you like that?'

'Yeah,' I say.

'A little? A lot?'

'A lot.'

'Less than on the slide, or more?'

'More,' I say.

'I've never done that for anyone. I've just invented it. But I enjoyed it too. I'll do it again one day.'

Then an idea pops into her head and she says:

'Do you want to touch it?'

I pretend to think about this new suggestion as I'm soft-pedalling. We arrive at the estate, there's the grass, at least what's left of it, like a green cloth ripped

31

to shreds. Touch her how, that's what I can't[1]

I cycle round the blocks, avoiding mine to keep away from my mother and my mates – I can see them from a distance but I don't think they can see us. She raises herself like before, this time by putting her foot on mine, I let go with my left hand, we're really getting our act together – I wouldn't mind if everyone could see the acrobatics at least, we should put this on at the end-of-year gala at Bouglione – and I slide my hand like a stalking animal in among the yellow, curly grass, without looking this time, just touching the top of the hair to the right and to the left, but then Lila says without laughing, she almost sounds serious:

'You're just in the bush there. You can go lower down, you know.'

I go lower down, I descend, the terrain starts to fold, split, I can feel the little tongue in the middle, she quivers all over when I touch it, then I don't know whether I should go left or right now, I hesitate, lower she says, there yes, push your finger in, I feel the flesh spread and open, I bend my finger a little and push, it goes in like it was making its own hole, it

_____

[1] This sentence is unfinished in the manuscript: probably 'what I can't work out'.

feels like damp moss, damp and warm too, and Lila, with her broken voice, almost sad-sounding, says:

'Yes, yes, like that, lie your finger along the length and put the tip in, just the tip, yes, rub it a bit, there, you're wanking me you naughty man.'

I do exactly what she says – every window on the estate has eyes for us, I'm thinking to myself. On the other hand I've never felt anything better than this, I tell myself as I write this here in my ruined dining room. You can rack your brains to find words that can say a hundredth of what you feel in a moment like that, your head and hand are powerless, because there are dreams as well, all the things that come into your mind, quickly quickly, her voice her hair her short sharp breaths, you even think about things you don't know about, it's a secret world, images appear in your head and you don't know where they come from, but it's contentment, it's a passing happiness you try to grab out of the air like a fly, that's how hard it is, it's actually more difficult, it lasts no time at all, then you've got hours of suffering trying to remember it. I'm sitting here in my demolished office writing draft after draft, which proves it. I cross out and I start again and I still don't get it right.

One thing I can say, this is the funny part, the bike started to lose speed (I'd stopped pedalling) and Lila, who's not completely out of it in spite of everything, says look out, we're going to fall. She lifts her foot, sits back on the crossbar, I quickly remove my hand, of course, I push the pedals round four or five times and I say:

'Do you want to do another tour?'

'You getting a taste for this?'

'How about you?' I say.

'I've got a bit of a sore bum,' she replies, 'but OK.'

I let go with my left hand to stick it back where it was before, but now Lila turns round to face me, lifts her eyes that I can only describe as the eyes of an angel, the eyes of the morning sky, and she asks me just like that:

'Have you got a hard-on?'

As if she was asking: is it raining, are you thirsty, do you want half of my chewing gum?

Totally natural, as simple as that.

I give a little shrug of the shoulders – like Little Maurice says, never admit anything to birds or cops. I make sure I don't answer her directly, as if the question, her aunt as well, she doesn't kiss me so that deep down I could only say.[1]

She puts it another way:

'Haven't you got a hard-on?'

I still think it's better not to reply.

So she lets go with her left hand, slides it behind her back, keeping her heavenly eyes on me, and finds my cock through my jeans, finds it straight away, no problem, my cock which is as hard as fuck, as you can imagine, stiff and miserable in its prison of thick cloth, and feeling the bump she says:

'I'd have been surprised if you hadn't.'

She smiles like only she knows how.

She holds the tip with four fingers, like when you're unscrewing the top of something, and she starts to stroke me; we're taking another turn round the estate, it's like she's trying to sharpen it, taper it, then suddenly she says:

'It must be suffering a bit in there. Do you want me to take it out?'

I do sometimes think about my cock. I say to myself that it's condemned to the shadows far from the sun, imprisoned for life with no hope of release; it doesn't know what it's guilty of. Maybe at the start of the

---

[1] A very obscure passage, with lots of crossings-out, reproduced here word for word.

world it was different, and cocks and pussies and bums were all left exposed, to sun, rain and wind as well. Maybe that's the feeling those Scandinavian nudists are trying to rediscover when they come here in the summer, to stay in camps. They're fenced in like everyone else – they'll be sending in humanitarian aid before long.

'Do you want me to?' she repeats.

'What?'

'Take it out.'

'You can't do it here.'

'Want to bet?'

'No.'

'Stand up a bit on the pedals, you'll see.'

I resist – I don't know why exactly, it's how I am, I'm not cool and macho, I'm not the type to piss in the street even if I'm dying to.

'You won't manage it.'

'You'll see.'

'My jeans are too tight.'

'What's the matter, you afraid?'

That's always the clincher. And any way, she assures me she'll sit right up close to me, she'll hide me under her dress, no one will see a thing even though it's lunchtime.

36

I get the bike moving again in a straight line, to take us past her block, I stand up on the pedals as she suggested. She gets my zip down no problem, her little white hand slips inside like five eels, I'm stiff fit to burst, it's not that easy getting the pants out of the way, it hurts my bits down below but finally she manages it, her hand gently grabs my cock, I've never felt anything like it, my cock which was all folded up unrolls spontaneously – hello open air, that's all it wanted, someone to take care of it. It's like an alien bursting out of a man's body, I don't recognise it, it's not part of me, it's a moving lump of meat, a surge of life, an explosion, it's got demands of its own.

Lila says:

'You see, it wants to.'

So she starts to stroke me with her thin fingers, it's unbelievable, she moves up and down, she sneaks a look, and her smile over her shoulder, she forms her fingers into a circle like a ring of flesh, and starts giving me a good wanking, at one point she removes her hand and puts her fingers in her mouth to dampen them. She asks me if it's good – I'm in no state to say no, I don't reply, how could I even manage to speak?

As we go past I see the Malian from Block C, the tall one who always wears dark glasses. He is crossing our path on his roller skates, this is how he takes his cat for a walk for an hour every day. He has his arm stretched out straight in front of him, supported by a strap, the elbow bent, the cat nestling peacefully on top of it with its eyes closed. They skate past quickly and don't notice anything – the Malian sees the world only through his cat, and when he takes it for a walk he sings softly to it in his own language.

When she closes her hand around me again she says:

'I'd like to suck you off but you can't do that on a bike.'

It's like she knows what she's talking about.

Then she lowers her voice and says:

'You can come, it's allowed. I'll bring you off, OK?'

And then, after a short pause:

'Just make sure we don't overbalance.'

She accelerates gently, with just three fingers now. Just below my stomach I feel a hollow, then a moment later it goes off, a hundred metres past the Campana it explodes like a pigeon's egg hitting a windscreen, I empty my pleasure into her hand which she has closed around the tip, she is still helping me, my whole body goes away, I am no longer anywhere, pleasure and happiness one and the same, her voice is coming from a distance, still telling me not to lose balance. They say that your heart misses one or two beats at times like this, like when you sneeze, I must have missed a few more, I've even closed my eyes, I can feel Lila tugging away gently to empty me completely, then she shakes her hand to get rid of it, her face is lit up, she sucks what's left of my come from her fingers, looking at me through her hair, I don't know if she's taking the piss, she sucks each finger greedily one by one, then she asks me if I liked it and I say yes.

'I'll tuck it back inside,' she says.

She does so and pulls up the zip at the same time, a little tap with her fingertips on my cock which is still hard and has trouble bending, then Lila says:

'Have you noticed we're outside your block? You should get off.'

I'd even forgotten we were on earth and I'm completely out of breath. I gently stop the bike, she hops down, I get off too, I take my bags and hand her the bike. I have this nagging feeling that I should say something, but I don't know what, the words only come to me later when I'm alone, at the time I'm usually tongue-tied, and this is a totally new situation anyway, I feel like a complete idiot. Lila acts natural as usual, she's even smiling and gracious. She takes the man's bike, places her left foot on the left pedal and pushes off with her right foot, the bike rolls forward, then she throws her right leg high over the saddle and I get a final flash, deliberate or not I don't know, her naked pussy, her nice pink and blonde slit, just long enough to draw breath, I'm stunned, one last secret, then she lowers it on to the front part of the saddle, the dress falls back and she starts pedalling straight away. But her legs are too short for the bike, or the saddle is raised too high, so she strikes a dancer's pose, in her usual white shoes, shouts bye over her shoulder, see you soon.

She goes and I stand there with my bags, the lighter for something she took in her hand and threw away.

Another day I meet her at the surgery, in the waiting room, she says hi Chimo how you doing when I sit down next to her – I go there every now and then to sell some blood.

'And how's things with you?' I say.

'All right.'

'You're not ill, are you?'

'I'm getting a prescription for my aunt.'

She doesn't say anything for a while, just stares into space, so I say: 'Does it bother you?'

'What?' she says.

'Me talking to you.'

'No,' she says, 'I was just thinking about something.'

'What about?'

'About giving someone a treat.'

I ask her what treat, she says: 'If I was in love with a man, I'd want him to see me fucking someone else.'

She doesn't even lower her voice.

'That's your treat?' I say.

'Or even with two other guys.'

'You think he'd like that?'

'I'm not sure, but I would.'

Then she doesn't say anything, I think she might have finished, but no. She starts again.

'I think it'd be a great treat to show him what I'm like when he fucks me. Because when you're fucking you can't really see properly, it just passes you by. But if he saw me once or twice, after that, whenever he fucks me, he'll remember what I do, what I'm like, and it'd really turn him on.'

'Who would you fuck with?' I ask.

'In front of my guy?'

'Yes.'

'With strangers,' she says, 'that's for sure. It'd be stupid to do it with friends or guys he might recognise, it'd just get really heavy, and anyway, I might like them better than him. I'd pick some guys off the street, there's plenty of them around, or some pros like the ones in porn films and I might make them wear a mask or a hood, so you wouldn't see their faces, they'd just be pieces of meat, you can give them any face you like. Lovely cocks without faces or names, that's how I imagine it, and I'd have a blindfold on too, that way you'd never recognise them if you bumped into them on the street, but every good-looking guy that goes past, it could be him.'

No good-looking guys in the vicinity here, just an old couple, the man is shaking, and a young guy from Block F, limp as a fillet of fish, he's so crazy one day the doc gave him a prescription, he said here take this, so when he left he ate the prescription. He's sitting there staring at the floor, picking his nose. Hello, anyone at home? His skull is a desert, the wells have dried up and the caravans have all gone.

I don't even know if anyone is listening to what we are saying.

So I ask Lila:

'Is that what love is to you?'

'Partly, yes,' she replies. 'What about you?'

'To be honest,' I say, 'I don't know what it is.'

'Have you never been in love?'

She hurts me with her blue eyes when she says this.

'I don't think so,' I say anyway.

'Aren't you sure?'

'No.'

'Neither am I,' she lobs back at me. 'But if I was in love, I tell you, it'd be a real treat.'

'And what if he didn't want it?'

'I'm sure he'd want it. Nine times out of ten he would.'

'I don't believe you,' I say.

'I'm telling the truth, Chimo. I always tell the truth, you know I do, I'm telling you I'd do it for him not for me. Because one thing's for sure, I wouldn't get off on it, not all the way at least.'

I say all the same I still can't really understand why she'd do it.

She taps her head with her finger and says:

'Because guys don't have much up here.'

She glances across at the idiot from Block F, who's sitting there with his mouth open, like a dead fish on a slab, still waiting for a shopper to buy him. As if she's trying to say: all guys are like that cretin over there.

The old man sitting to the side shakes more and more, he's shaking so much you expect his buttons to fall off. His wife touches his arm from time to time and makes a tutting sound with her tongue. When she touches him he shakes too, it must be catching.

'Their heads are full of mush, Chimo. You've got no idea. They don't think about anything, they don't dream about anything any more.'

She's right, I often tell myself, the moment you

stop dreaming is when you're not a kid any more, you can see it's not worth it, your life isn't going to change, it's going to be like this for ever, you've got nothing but your hand to wipe away your tears.

Then she says:

'A guy gets it together with a girl, and whether she likes it or not he just rams it in hard, like a dog digging a hole to find a buried bone, it's no use calling him or pulling his tail, he's digging away like mad, he's out of breath, he can't hear anything, but if you only knew all the gentle things you can do, Chimo, touching, caressing, foreplay, talking dirty, but mainly the thought that you're doing it, that it's you doing it, that it's your arsehole being penetrated by a big cock, just knowing that it's you adds to the pleasure, it's incredible.'

'Why?' I ask.

'I don't know why,' she replies. 'I really like looking at myself in a mirror when I'm sucking off or when I'm being screwed, I think I've already told you, but the girl I can see in the mirror has no feelings, she's just drawn on the glass, she's cold, it's as if it's not me, then sometimes I pull the sheet or something else over the head of the guy who's screwing me, so I only see the bit of him I need and that's enough.

Guys are so closed up you wonder sometimes if they've lost the key. You want to tell them to open up a bit, let some air in upstairs, but they don't even have an upstairs. That's why when I'm with my own guy, the one I'd be in love with, I'd like to help him, feed his mind, so he can have some images in the bank, a whole bag of images, a film he can screen when he wants, that'd get him hard pretty quick and give him a great orgasm every time, that's what I call a treat.'

She often sets off talking like that, never pausing for breath, you get the feeling she could churn it out for hours at a time. The things that go on in her head, they're almost frightening, but at the same time you don't want her to stop because, honestly, it's like life is transformed into something else in her mouth and it makes me ravenous, like a flea on a goat's head.

'And what about you?' I say.

'What do you mean?'

'If you loved a guy would you like it if he screwed other girls in front of you just to give you a treat?'

'I'd love it,' she says, half closing her eyes, 'especially if they wore masks so I couldn't recognise them, real sluts, nymphos who'd devour his balls, his arse, who'd give him a gigantic erection and then stick it in

46

themselves right to the base. I'd store all that in my image bag, it'd turn me on like nobody's business, just talking about it's making me wet.'

At that moment the door opens and the doc comes out with some fat old dear who's crying and he calls for the next person, who is the idiot from Block F. It takes him a moment to realise it's his turn, the shaking man's wife has to say, I think it's you, then it's like he's leapt out of a dream without a parachute, he jumps up and walks quickly over to Lila, with feverish eyes, then says, like three short sneezes:

'Slut slut slut!'

Then he goes in with the doc who closes the door without passing comment, seeing as how it's nothing to do with him. The old shaker carries on shaking, just his wife gives us a look, but not for very long, she just zaps us and that's it.

Lila says:

'Did you see that twat?'

'He was listening to us,' I say.

'Got what he deserved, the wanker. Did you see his eyes? Born brain-dead like a lot of them, and he's not showing signs of improvement. Before you know it you've got a killer on your hands. It ties in with what I was saying to you, Chimo: when a girl loves a man she has to help him. On their own they're not whole, they're stuck in a rut and they're dangerous, they live in a tunnel and the trains have stopped running.'

'Are you sure you'd really like it?' I ask her. 'If the guy of your dreams was bonking other girls in front of you?'

'I'm not saying all the time. But once in a while, definitely.'

'Wouldn't you be jealous?'

'Oh no.'

'What if it was better with the others than with you?'

'I'd be surprised,' she says.

'You never know.'

This silences her for a moment, then she says:

'Thing is, I've already got some images in stock, some really nice ones, but you can never have enough, never, besides they wear out and become faint, you have to renew them. I'd love to have images of hell, with the squelch of fucking and the smell of sperm, all red and black with a touch of white flesh as well. Oh I'd want the man of my heart seen to by witches, juicy, red-hot whores who would kill him, drive him wild. If he did that for me, if he gave me this treat, oh I'd be crazy for him, I swear.'

'Do you know any girls who'd do that for you?'

'Yes, you can find them,' she says, 'there are sluts all over the place. But the best thing would be to pay them, ones who'll do anything, real wild ones. It gets me dreaming, Chimo, if only you knew. And deep down lots of women are like me, they'll never tell you like I do, they don't dare, but it stirs them up inside, you've no idea.'

'If you like it so much, why don't you do it?' I ask.

Still staring at me with her light blue eyes, she says:

'Like, where do I find this guy to be in love with?'

I'm now going to write about the shock I got. Even in a place like this, the Oak Tree estate, you think you know everyone, then all of a sudden you see someone you didn't even know existed until then, like Lila. Where did she come from? Some people say that she's been here since she was a kid, that she was born here, but when she was little no one noticed her with her satchel and her knitted woollen hat; she opened like a flower one day, the next day there she was. Now she hits you between the eyes, you see nothing but her. And others say that's not right, she arrived less than three months ago, her mother snuffed it at Villejuif hospital and left her to her sister, the aunt, who lived here already, we know that, and so they talk till they're blue in the face – if you can't agree about something as simple as a girl, then the world of war and politics must be way beyond you. No one really knows about Lila: yes yes she arrived on foot with a suitcase on wheels; no no I knew her at school, even at the age of seven or eight she drew things in her exercise book that would make you blush; yes yes she arrived at seven o'clock one October evening, she came along here, scraping her suitcase along the ground, and so on and so on. It just shows that even if you never leave your home turf where you know everyone by their nicknames, Nettle-eye Mélie or slippery Mouloud, the truth is you don't know anyone really, they all escape you, at least the ones who interest you. Like a Gruyère has holes they've got their secrets, you too probably.

Lila has changed my life. To start with, I can't imagine the estate without her. The place has no centre without her. Even if she's not there, she's there. I couldn't get her out of my life, I couldn't do anything without her. I'd have to suck my brain out with a straw, with all the poison there is in there. For once the light has come to the Oak Tree, a piece of sky has moved in over us, for once you've got something that is something different.

She's better than the lot of them, even the ones you see on the telly, the old face-lifts on *Dynasty*, the trussed-up turkeys wind-surfing in their pretty swimsuits on *Malibu*, those stupid mannequins, OK they're good-looking, but they cross their legs like octopuses, they look so much the same they're like soldiers on parade, they're such snobs, take a good look you little idiots, watch me walk on by. You can bet their pussies are dry, all these women you see on the box, even Vanessa, even Merlene Ottey, the thirty-five-year-old sprinter who climbs into her blocks with the most gorgeous arse in the world (that's not just for running with, that's for sure), every single last one of them pales into insignificance next to her, and another thing, another thing, oh yes, near or far, she looks you in the eye hi how you doing I'm fine, you reach out your hand and you touch her, she's real, she's the local delight, our home-grown beauty and nobody else's, and that way she has of talking and the things she says.

Even before the day on the slide she was putting it about a bit with her pussy, so it seems. Mouloud says he met her one evening, she says hi how are you, and at the same time through her dress you could see her feeling herself. Another time you say something to her she replies I'm rubbing myself off, just to be crude on purpose, or else to sound like a boy. At the surgery she comes out with this orgy with headless men, saying it's not faces that excite her but

52

cocks, it's making love with anonymous men and she says all this without blinking, as if she was talking about a passing bird. She's an angel with the mouth of a whore – you'd think the words that crossed her lips would do her harm, that her teeth would fall out with the shame, but they don't, it's like a light summer breeze, nothing gets broken and it even caresses you a little.

Before I talk about this shock I'll talk about love round here, just to fill you in. On the estate everyone has sex from the age of fifteen, but not as much as you might think. The first time, you get off with the most experienced girl – there are always one or two who aren't necessarily top of the range, they help all the boys to lose their virginity and then they get married. But later on, when the boys are about seventeen or eighteen, the boys can go weeks without a shag and you can see it really gets to them. So they take some girl into a cellar and a gang of them have their way with her. The girl may or may not know what to expect; once she's down in the cellar with a bit of grass she goes all the way, sometimes she yells and she cries but sometimes she'll do it again. Apart from one time ages ago I find it hard to join in because I really don't want to, so I just watch and pretend I'm enjoying it, but it's once every six months, no more.

And you have to take care these days with this virus that's going round, because the condom dispenser on the estate is always empty, some guys pinch the lot on the first day and then sell them at a knock-down price.

It's normal for girls and married women too to turn tricks, especially on Thursday evenings and Friday afternoons when they're skint at the end of the month – in other words, all the time – also teenagers to pay for their studies or meals at the university refectory, even minors. Their husbands and fathers turn a blind eye, it's either that or total ruin. They leave the flat for three or four hours and when they get back everything is sorted.

Their clients are sometimes guys from the estate, but mainly they come from Paris on the bus or the RER. They aren't that well off either, that's why they come out here for sex; it's fifty francs a go – amateur stuff, but a fuck all the same. Once in a while smart-looking guys drive over here looking for little African virgins, and round here there's nothing but, they make them every week with sheep's membrane and a bit of nail varnish. These smart guys must have their doubts, since they bring double-strength condoms with them.

On the estate there are lots of women without pimps who work on a casual basis, but some of it's more organised, it's part of the rackets run by former pros of thirty or forty. That mainly goes on in the cellars, with rugs, cushions, hi-fis – the lot. It doesn't last long of course, this trip to the Orient, this dip into the secret world of the harem, but it's something you can make the most of a long time afterwards if you embroider it a bit.

It's fuck market day here on Thursday afternoons when the weather's good. The guys queue up outside the blocks, they bring chairs or they play boules or dominoes. The girls come out in their home-made sexy dresses to get them excited, it's a sight worth seeing, we call it the tit 'n' bum parade. Every now and then a guy leaves his dominoes and goes down into the cellar with one of them; sometimes when he comes back the others applaud, the horniest ones manage ten to twelve guys a week, even off-duty cops, it's not unknown. There's supposed to be a gay version, they still do the little Arab boy bit, but not round here – round here queers tend to be frowned on, I don't know why, even more so in the southern suburbs, in Bagneux and Créteil as well.

In short, love round here is like everything else, you make do with what you've got, you get by. I'm saying this to explain how Lila fits in to all this. No one has ever seen Lila sell herself to anyone. She's set apart from everyone else. Most Fridays she stays at home watching telly with her aunt, you don't see her with the other girls, and then she goes away for two or three days, who knows where.

Lila.

Now, about this shock I got.

Leaving aside the slide and particularly the bike, this is the way it is: I must be the only person she talks to apart from her aunt. I thought she must talk to the others like she did with me, but no. I asked them yesterday, Ruben the Armenian, Mouloud, Big Jo: does Lila say things to you? They said no, never. They give her some chat when she goes by, like the other girls, she never replies, or hardly at all.

'She's a stuck-up bitch,' says Mouloud. 'She looks right past you, she doesn't notice you. You don't exist as far as she's concerned.'

'Does she speak to you?' Little Maurice asks me.

'Yeah, she does sometimes.'

'Does she tell you stuff?'

'Yeah,' I say.

'What stuff?'

'Oh, nothing,' I say cautiously.

'If she says nothing she should keep her mouth shut.'

'Yeah, you're right,' I say.

'She's just a stupid cow,' Gilbert concludes.

They leave, they're not in a good mood.

I stay behind. It's the shock. She only talks to me. Of all the young guys on the estate, she only talks to me, Chimo. The rest are a bunch of zombies, they don't exist. Only to me.

I want to say this: it's not even the fact that, after the moment of ecstasy on the bike, I would think about fucking her, or even holding her hand one night, or even kissing her behind her ear or wherever, or stroking her shoulders, holding her round the waist, all those things you see people do in films, thoughts I can't prevent running through my heart and my belly, especially at night when I'm in bed and I can hear my mother snoring; they keep coming back, with my eyes closed I can see her gestures, so I get up quiet as a spider and creep off to the kitchen to write and that calms me down. It's not even that I think about that like it's a dream that might come true one day. Oh no, she's still an unexplored land, you're sailing by, Chimo, you can see her from afar, but at least she sees you and talks to you. Now why does she say the things she says and not a word about anything else? And also why does she show herself to me and why did she make me come in her hand, why me and no one but me, when there's a big wide world out there. It's tearing me apart, I'm racking my brains and no light appears.

I've also got to say this: when I first started writing, years ago now, it was like I was writing an essay: I wrote the storyline of a film I had seen on the telly, how dumb can you get, or I wrote about how sad I was all the time, or an accident in the street, a fight. I once wrote a story with vampires in a dark castle. Other stories, once I'd started them I never knew how to finish them, even on the first page they'd be getting on my nerves, I'd tell myself if that one gets on your nerves what about the others, so I'd end up burning the pages in the sink and pouring water on top, then I'd go back to bed in despair.

My mother works at the town hall as a cleaner. It's a job-creation scheme; she gets up at five, summer or winter, sometimes I hadn't even got to sleep when I'd hear her get up, talking quickly in a low voice – I've never managed to hear what she says, maybe prayers – she'd leave in a hurry and I'd stay there with my lost night.

For a long time I had to get up at seven myself to take my little sister to school. Now she goes on her own and I sleep in. Whether I sleep or not makes no difference, the day comes anyway. I feel as useless as a chair on the ceiling, the others down below prop up the walls in case they fall. I remember once at school the teacher asking Little Maurice what he wanted to do later, he replied: something or other.

But since Lila spoke to me for the first time, the session on the slide, a dam has burst inside me. The following night I realised that I could write about it easily, that there was no need to make up vampires and such like in my head, that Lila is there, she is looking at me and telling me things in her own peculiar way with those eyes you can hide nothing from. I never thought of writing porn with arses and cocks and words like that. At first it wasn't easy, it troubled me, I'm not the exhibitionist type, and it made me feel ashamed, since my mother is totally strict about that sort of thing, and now it just flows like water on a rainy day, it's like Lila was moving my hand, her voice sings in my head for hours afterwards. Whether it's porn or not I don't know any more, the pen just slides across the paper, driven by an invisible engine, I've already reached the end of one notebook and I'm innocent, I've got nothing to blame myself for, and I don't get annoyed any more when I write; I can do two pages an hour, especially when the memories are fresh as eggs, and when I go back to bed I fall asleep.[1]

I admit I even thought of writing her a poem, but I don't know how, I'm afraid it might turn out all soppy and stupid. I remember something I was told when I was small, it must have been an African thing: in the black night a black table a little black ant, God can see it.

To which I'd add: God can see the ant, but he doesn't see me.

I had even planned to write her a filthy poem, to give her a bit of what she likes, only, I couldn't write it. When it comes from me I can't do it, it's weird.

All the same I have to wonder why she tells me

---

[1] The first notebook ends here. It is dated 19 September 1995. The second notebook seems to pick up exactly where this leaves off.

this since she doesn't know I write. I'd like to say it's to turn me on, but it's not simple, because she really is a nice girl, at least I think so, she's not just some cockteaser. But I just can't believe she flashed at me. I mean I'm not exactly ugly, knock-kneed and pasty-faced, but I'm no Clint Eastwood either, nor Stallone for that matter, with his drooping eyes. Apparently he's got a minute dick, that's what his ex-wife told the press. No I'm your average suburban type, dark and curly, of course, with dark eyes, they say the dark-skinned type is getting more and more widespread throughout the world, there'll soon be no blonds left, another reason why Lila's a rarity. You'll be telling me that you can always dye your hair and even lighten your skin like Michael Jackson with a pumice stone and stuff from the chemist that works deep down, but his kids'll still be black if he has any. One day the punks came down here from Bobigny, just to strut around, probably, and I thought: you can stick a Mohican on your head and dress like a shiny crow, you're still the same underneath.

This is when I realise I can't write, I lose my way all the time, I start a sentence then I wander off, I cross out, I set off at tangents, I come back, and I end up lost. I have to reread what I've written to find out where I started from. I reckon people that write have plans like architects, then they only have to fill in the houses, they know where they're going, it's a trade they've learned. I just pull on my poor string the best I can. It's not the feelings or ideas I can't find, it's the words. I pinch money from my mother, a franc here and there, so I can buy myself a dictionary one day, then I'll learn it by heart, but until then there are lots of things I feel which I can't find the right expression for, it drives me mad sometimes, how did other people learn how to do it? The people round here, the guys and girls, white or not, make do with a pitiful excuse for a language, with their ums and ers and yeah, OK, and fucking this and poxy that, they've said all there is to say in their cage of words. Of course I bust a gut trying not to write like they speak, then I copy it all out here. Even rhyming slang is a drag, it's limited, but I'm not sure I've got it right. Not everyone has got the same words at their fingertips. You always feel like you're at sea and there's this green island you don't go near. It's guarded better than the Bank of France, it's covered in all types of magnificent fruit: words which people feast on. It's like plundering a treasure chest in a tropical paradise. But not you, never you,

you stick to your galley, put your back into it and row, you little shit. What are you raising your head for? You can't look over the side or listen to the beautiful songs from over there. Feel the lash and keep your mouth shut.

Excluded, that's what they say. They drone on and on about it. Fuck me, they have conferences about it and everything. But you never know what you're excluded from. From Santa Barbara? From those places you see on the telly with their swimming pools and bright blue topless bikinis? But these places are on another planet, there's no way they're on earth, it's fantasy world – the movie. Even their sun is artificial. We never have fine weather here. The blocks keep the fine weather out. Sometimes it gets quite hot, oppressive even, but it's never fine. Fine is something else entirely.

Not far from here there's an estate that you could confuse with ours or any other, they call it Shady Nook – but Little Maurice, who's got family there, says it's the buildings that overshadow the trees.

The trees are just like us, stuck here like objects without knowing why, like us unable to move, you'll probably say it's the same for all trees, but it's worse for them, they're in all this ugliness, this grey sun, they all have to be forced, and they're all the same, no variety at all, no bushes or flowers because of the vandals, a tree every fifteen metres in a straight line. My mother says when she sets off early in the morning, if the wind's blowing she can hear them cry.

But my mother hears tears everywhere.

It's true that round here with all the rackets that go on you can get whatever you want at knock-down prices – tellies, mopeds, DJs' record decks, weapons from Israel, brought in God knows how, Nikes and Reeboks with three stripes down the side, the really classy ones. In some of the cellars, or even in people's rooms, they set up black market dens, modern souks. People come from Paris to buy their hi-fis and designer gear, booze from every country, jewellery, cigars, furniture, Apple Macs with printers at a third of the normal price. The rackets bring in good money, but it's restricted to the chosen few. Usually it works by families, cousins mainly, or by contacts made in prison, and there are risks attached. None of us round here are cut out to be gangsters, even if we dream about it at night – it seems like an easy life compared to the alternative, which is to be completely, utterly skint.

I've even dreamed about marrying Lila. I say dreamed, because poverty's my middle name, I haven't even got four francs to buy flowers, never mind a wedding ring, a dress, plus tickets and hotels for the honeymoon. It's like some soap opera, Chimo in Malibu, a cloud that drifts past without raining on the dry ground. Maybe it doesn't have any rain in its belly, or the courage you'd need to marry an angel like her, with all those snakes of words that slither out of her mouth, and of course she does these disappearing acts for two or three days at a time, even her aunt doesn't know where she is. I know it'd be a huge risk, leaving the house in the morning to go to work (as if) and leaving Lila all alone, it'd eat away at me all day long. I sometimes imagine her now in the middle of an orgy, bristling with cocks like a pin-cushion, and I turn up unexpected one afternoon – what a nightmare, it's too painful to think about.

They also ask you questions about drugs: so, do you young people take anything? Like, what do we buy the gear with, it doesn't grow on trees. All right, every now and again you take a few puffs on a joint, but the next stage up is for rich people, you need the dough or else you have connections and deal

65

yourself, which is not my cup of tea.

Round here, apart from the few who run the rackets, people have so little that my mother buys second-hand bread. People don't know these things, you have to tell them. Lucette, the Martinican who lives downstairs and gets a pension from the Post Office buys bread on Monday, say, lives on it for two days, and on Wednesday my mother buys what's left at half price and that does us for another couple of days.

We've got nothing. The only mopeds we have are the ones we nick, then you go round the block three times and run out of petrol. And the funny thing is, when you are able to move, you stay put – I've often noticed this. Why go anywhere else, you say. To do what? You don't look as shabby if you stay here, where at least everyone else is the same, as you would gallivanting around the countryside. Everyone can see through you, when you've got nothing in your pockets people can see it in your eyes.

And now that she is here, now she says all this to me, and that I'm the only one she talks to, nothing defeats me any more. I don't give a toss about Santa Barbara. I don't know if I can expect anything else, it'd be weird if it happened one day, I must be crazy, weird, weird, weird, weird, the word whistles in my ear. Everything she gives me is good, the world is dark apart from her.

I am sitting at home sorting out some lentils – we buy them in bulk from a Tunisian – when I hear my name called out, I put my head out of the window and I see her waving at me to come down. I tell my mother I'll be back soon and I go down.

On the stairs I meet the Algerian from the sixth floor with his son, they're trying to push a fat sheep up the steps by hitting it round the backside. The sheep seems to have different ideas, it's putting up some resistance; maybe he thinks there's going to be a party but it won't be his, that they're going to slit his throat in the bath like they've done with others.

I go outside, Lila's moved further away, she's sitting upright on a patch of bare lawn and looking at the tips of her feet. I go over and say hello. She's moving her feet backwards and forwards, which makes the muscles of her legs flex and unflex. I've heard that when she was younger she used to do gymnastics, which explains her skills on the bike, but one day

68

she had a nasty fall, so she walked out and that was that.

Her muscles are still supple and pretty, you'd never get tired of looking at them.

She doesn't return my greeting straight away, she seems in a sulky mood today, I wait for a bit, but not too long, I flop down on the yellow grass next to her.

'What's wrong?' I say.

'Nothing,' she replies.

'Do you want to tell me something?'

'What me? No.'

'Why did you call me down then?'

'I can't remember.'

I haven't said anything to put her in a bad mood. I just wait.

She started wiggling the tips of her still very clean white shoes again and stares at them, as if there was nothing in the world as interesting as her pumps. I tell you, in situations like this I never know how to act. I'm not outgoing by nature, and on top of that, this girl drags me in her wake, she shakes me up, I'm like putty in her hands. What the hell am I doing, I'm saying through clenched teeth. You call the little dog and he comes scampering down, I tell myself off as much as I can without making a sound.

Haven't even got a cigarette to offer her.

I summon up my courage and ask her:

'What are you thinking about?'

I'm already slightly scared of what she might say.

'Same as usual,' she says.

'What's that then?'

'I'm thinking about having a cock up my pussy.'

For all I try to see it coming, it throws me every time, it catches me unawares. I suddenly feel naked in a forest full of animals, sharp teeth and poison all around, I feel anxious, it's the thrill, my tongue's in a knot but I ask:

'And you wanted to talk to me?'

'Maybe, Chimo. I was on my own.'

She called me Chimo, at least that proves she knows I'm here.

After a short pause, she says without looking at me:

'Maybe, I don't know.'

I record everything even the silences, at times like this I'm a perfect machine. At other times I'm distracted, people talk to me and I'm miles away, they say Chimo goes away in his head, but not with her, never.

I turn slightly towards her and I see that Lila on

the dry grass has become a sort of picture, like the ones you see in books of fairy stories. I had one when I was a kid, the princess was lost in thought, it said, or the deserving but ill-favoured girl. She's a sort of orphan and victim of cruelty like in *Les Misérables* on the telly – I enjoyed that – but resigned and brave, 'I keep my troubles to myself', just flicking a quick glance in my direction.

I'm even embarrassed writing this, I feel like such a stupid kid sometimes.

'I'm here,' I say.

'I know you are. Chimo?'

'Yeah, what?'

'Have you thought about what I said to you?'

'Yes, I've thought about it.'

I didn't dare say that for the last few days I haven't thought about anything else for a single moment, each time it does my head in more.

'And?'

'And nothing,' I say.

She shrugs her shoulders, but not out of contempt, or irritation, I think it's because I discourage her, I don't keep up with her, then she falls into a heavy silence and finally she says:

'I find it's not enough for me. Doing it's good but

it's not enough. There's something missing, I don't know what. I'd really like to see at the same time as I try things, but it's not comfortable. Day before yesterday when I was fucking I tried it with a mirror, but the mirror was too small, I twisted my shoulders but in the end I couldn't see anything and I lost all the enjoyment of the fuck. And the guy couldn't understand what I was trying to do, he wasn't that bright, bit of a brute, but a huge cock – very, very nice, a Christian cock as well, with nothing chopped off, that's how I like them, with that little bridle underneath and slightly curved. I hardly saw it at the start before he put it in, it's a shame. There are some things it's not fair to hide.'

'That's true,' I say, though I haven't a clue why I say it, I think I probably sound stupid.

She bends right forward until her forehead touches her knees and she says:

'I'd really love to have some photos or even a video. And have a quiet look at it afterwards. I'd really love that.'

'Yes,' I say, still sounding stupid, but I always feel stupid when I'm with her.

She stands up stretching her muscles – she's definitely got a touch of the acrobat about her – and

72

she says, looking at me straight in the face:

'Chimo, could you do me a favour?'

'What?' I say.

'Could you film me while I'm fucking?'

She has this knack of asking the very question I least expect.

'I've never filmed anything before,' I say at once.

'It's not hard, you know.'

'But I've never done it.'

'These new cameras are totally automatic. You just have to get in the right position to see properly.'

'To see what?' I ask.

As I write this I realise she can be a really cruel girl. I didn't feel like that at the time, but now I do.

'To see what?' she repeats like she's talking to an idiot. 'To see my pussy when he sticks it in, of course, or my arse, or both, with my head in the shot at the same time if possible, or at least my eyes to prove that it's really me. You're a friend, aren't you, you'd do that for me?'

'I don't know – yes.'

'Yes or no?'

'Yes,' I say.

'Can you find a camera?'

'I can ask around.'

'These guys put the idea in my head not so long ago and I can't get rid of it. It makes me wet to think about it.'

'What guys?' I say.

'Some guys who were scouting round the north suburb.'

'Scouting for what?'

'For porn films.'

I feel myself swirling round like dirty water in a sink, being sucked into a bottomless hole, I can't grab hold of anything and I'm falling, falling.

She talks more quickly now; she's getting carried away and becomes more animated. She says all this:

'They go all the way these days, but they insist on no condoms. That puts a lot of people off. But they say that because of AIDS people hardly ever fuck around these days, and don't do it more at home, less if anything, so the thing is they want to watch other people fucking. They want other people to take the risk for them, you see? And the more disgusting it is, the more they want it, blood and violence as well, everything they won't do themselves any more. And everything totally visible, no pretending and fake orgasms, whip-marks and everything. So there's a fortune in porn films, especially amateur ones,

74

because they're not trying to be artistic, you can see it's real life. With the element of risk as well, death at the end of a cock, but for someone else. You can wank off in comfort, you watch them fucking and you say to yourself: if he's HIV positive, then he's infected that big blonde.'

She continues, she's in full swing:

'They find guys and girls who are out of work or on the streets, they put them in some gaff somewhere which they've decked out with cushions and rugs, everyone fucks on cue and they film it. It takes as long to film as it does to do it, then it's so long, see you around. Apparently the film-makers never fuck, as a precaution, same way the big dealers never shoot up. Apparently before the virus it was usual in hard-core films for the actress to give the cameraman a blow-job at the end of the day – not any more. It saves time as well, business comes first, they make two films a day, did you know that? They've got these pills from Burma or wherever which give you a hard-on when required and a special liquid for extra lubrication when necessary. Apparently it's sometimes girls behind the camera, they are always the most extreme, they shout orders: do this do that; no pretending; open wider you whore; stick your tongue right up his arse; you two guys fuck her at the same time; stop complaining; go on hit her, hit her again harder, if she cries out it's because she loves it, I want to hear her cry out, come on, it's the woman behind the camera who calls the shots. And you, the couple who are fucking, aren't allowed to argue, or else you're out of there and you don't get paid. They make a packet, you know, Chimo. They say it's a global market, especially for natural blondes like me, in spite of the competition from Russia – the Poles as well, there's loads of sluts over there. The clients are choosy about the colour, I've learned that much. For example, the Japanese don't want any blacks – I'd never have known that, but it's true – and no over-large dicks either, so the viewers don't feel too small. These amateur films are made fast, you can reckon on two or three a day. But they sell them all round the world, you wouldn't believe it, the Eskimos have got loads of them, and they carry them across the Sahara in caravans. And with blondes it's that much better, seems everyone adores them, seeing as how the white race is disappearing – we're dying out, Chimo, not you but me – so they go mad in Africa when they see that it's a real blonde, like when a girl washes her pussy with soap and it stays blonde. Then with all these laser disc thingies and CD Roms, all these new gadgets, any girl who's not ugly and lazy and isn't saving her pussy for her handsome prince, can make two or three thousand francs in cash a day, it's better than dealing. What am I saying, a day? In an afternoon or evening. Two or three grand just for fucking, just think about it.'

Her words stop there on the edge of her mouth. You'd think she'd been in a dream of her own and now it's over.

Her silence is as loud as when she speaks.

I ask her:

'Have you done it?'

She shakes her head, just once.

'Are you sure?' I say.

'What are you, my brother?' she says.

'No,' I say.

Then she says:

'I told them I was a virgin and I wanted four grand. They said they'd think about it.'

'What if they see that you're not a virgin?'

'They won't,' she says.

Then she looks at me and asks me again:

'Why do I get wet just thinking about it?'

'What, you seeing yourself or other people seeing you?'

'Both. Especially me seeing myself.'

I tell her I don't know why, it's beyond me, and that's true. But I'm unable to refuse her the favour of filming her, though to be honest, I'm scared. I'd be too afraid that she'd turn her back on me and never speak to me again and I'd lose her for ever.

She could ask me to do lots of things, and she knows it, lots and lots, even something stupid. Her eyes, her mouth – I'd just say yes, yes. There's no other word that will do for her. Today she's wearing a blue hairband to hold her hair back in a sort of karate style, which shows off her pale forehead more, there's a little, narrow vein winding down the side, it's her blood flowing inside, it's a river seen from the air in a geography book, an atlas, a blue vein flowing towards paradise.

Then she says again:

'It's just that it's not enough to do it, to feel the cock, it's not enough, I have to see it as well. I don't know if you can understand. You have to see that it's you, you, who's doing it, that's it's really you with this tool inside you. It heightens the pleasure, it's deeper, better, it's like you're doing it with two guys,

78

one right there and the other in the mirror, and you almost feel ashamed.'

I find it funny that feeling ashamed should give her pleasure, but I don't say anything.

Every time I'm with her I realize the huge number of things I don't know, even though she's younger than me.

She turns to me again, she asks me:

'Will you do it, then?'

'I'll have to find a camera first.'

'Can you find one quickly?'

'Where will we do it?'

'I'll let you know. I don't know myself yet. It depends.'

I've now got to give you a few details about life round here.

Obviously I can only get hold of a camera if I pinch one, or get someone else to pinch one and lend it to me, but I'd need to pay him and I don't have anything. Something like that doesn't stay around for long, the fences soon get their hands on them, they have these little secret markets, what we call back-of-a-lorry sales, Sunday markets with music and majorettes or simple street-corner things, it's more or less the same circuit as for radios, cars and second-hand hi-fis. Of course it's all at a tenth of the price, which still leaves a margin, but everyone takes their cut along the way, and in any case the fences snap them up quickly, I mean that they won't be on offer weeks later, they're not difficult to shift, they don't keep them in stock.

You can always have a quiet word, see if a friend of a friend has the item here or somewhere else, but it's very rare to find it the day you need it. Especially if, like our little gang here, you don't frequent the higher circles. You have to look around for the item, or you can place an order and make an offer.

Little Maurice knows an antique dealer near Beauvais who has a sort of catalogue with photos of pieces of furniture, vases and things, colour photos. He shows it to his customers and they choose something – I want that, I'll have that painting there – only he doesn't have these items in his shop, they're still in their owners' houses, this guy has done a sort of recce, so to speak, and when someone likes a piece, when he has agreed a sale and taken a deposit even, he sends a gang round to nick it. It's highly organised, he says it's not worth nicking anything if you're not sure you're going to sell it. One time, according to Maurice, though he tends to make things up, this guy offered an old commode in his catalogue to the owner himself, who recognised it straight away. There was one hell of a slanging match – but that's my commode I tell you – with the police and everything, but it was all finally sorted out, the dealer switched the photo or something like that, the guy withdrew his complaint and apologised for the fuss – think nothing of it, sir, anyone can make a mistake, believe me – they even drank some champagne together, parted as friends, and the following weekend they nicked his commode, which is now on a farm in Canada with four or five other bits and pieces.

We aren't in that league, we're small fry.

As for making some regular money, here are a few ways:

Sell some blood at the surgery, no more than once a month, like I've already said, but you get next to nothing for blood.

Help to tidy the graves in the cemetery before All Saints, that's an idea that came from Marseille, but it's only seasonal.

Convince the girls that the fashion is for short hair, so they have it cut and you can sell it for wigs.

Occasionally in the autumn gather leaves for the town hall, or clean up the pigeon shit in the squares.

Carry the old folks' shopping upstairs for them

when the lifts are out of order, in other words more or less the whole time. Also take their rubbish down, those that don't chuck it out the window – but all the old folk are skint.

Sell your spunk at the sperm bank, but that's only once a year, because there's too much competition, everyone wants to wank off for twenty-five francs.

Get hold of the skins of sheep that have had their throats cut – a Polish furrier in Pantin buys them at sixty francs a skin.

Collect broken toys from children and fix them up to sell at the flea market, but that takes a bit of work and the Pakistanis are on to it too.

Pick grass and sell it to people who own rabbits, but they often do it themselves; also sell on rabbit skins.

Collect offcuts from the butcher and mince them up for cat food, but you need equipment for that and it's a lot of work for very little.

You can see that doesn't get you very far and so you soon turn to crime, to theft. And anything's worth nicking, because everything can be sold, more or less. Last year a gang in Aubervilliers specialised in ripping off the shoes from the entrances of mosques around the area, especially trainers, ones that are easy to sell, they even sent them off to Africa and Iran, where there's a shortage, but the imams bought cupboards and padlocks, so that was the end of that.

You can also play the gigolo, all the boys dream about that: a nice fat white woman aged forty or even fifty, totally loaded, looking for a weekly poke, but you can fantasise about that your whole teenage years and never get your rocks off.

You can also sit under the table with your mouth open waiting for crumbs, you get dole after six years. In the meantime a commission for carrying some dodgy items or keeping a lookout for the dealers when they're on their rounds, or nicking tyres, aerials, headlights – anything that's out of doors is exposed, it can disappear just like that – even dogs on leads, cats on windowsills, for vivisection, or you can clear out a shop window on nights where there's a spot of communal smash and grab.

That's doesn't happen very often and you can easily get yourself shot. So instead you go for the stuff that comes along, in other words mainly women's bags, either with or without a razor to cut the straps. The trick is to snatch the thing and scarper quickly. Usually you chuck the bag to a mate, and sometimes to another one again, like in rugby, it's a passing game.

The entrances to banks are a good place for that, shops as well and bus ticket machines, where there's almost nothing in the vicinity, the drivers don't give a toss, but it's best at night when they're going home and it's getting dark. You wait for them in pairs on the pavement outside a door, you stand there chatting innocently. It's got to be some other part of town – even Paris is OK, but Paris has got its own gangs, they guard their own patch – so there you are, two or three metres from the door, you don't know the code, of course, you see the woman arrive – always better if she's alone, coming back from a meal out, the theatre, she's had a bit too much to drink, she's sleepy, just thinking about her white sheets – you let her tap in the code, you look casual, you chat and make sure you don't look her way, so she opens the door and goes in. But the neat thing is, now there are codes, the doors take five or six seconds to close again. You make a dash for it, the entrance hall is usually dark, you grab the bag, the woman screams, but it's mainly fear and panic, she's frozen, rooted to the spot, you're already out the door, in the street you and your mate run off in opposite directions, you've already arranged to meet up somewhere an hour later.

In well-off neighbourhoods you always get about five or six hundred francs a bag, sometimes the odd piece of jewellery, but that's not very often – these days costume jewellery is mainly paste. You can sell credit cards and passports in Bobigny for next to nothing. The rest, keys, handkerchiefs and all that make-up crap they accumulate we chuck away. That just leaves the bag, which might be a designer make, in which case it gets sold on through a specialist market, sometimes disguised, and ends up in Belgium or Italy in the hands of street sellers.

It can be a bit of a let-down sometimes, I tell you, but there's still nothing like the excitement you feel when you open the bag each time. There's always something unexpected: glasses, postcards, a piece of cheese, even a joint on a couple of occasions, designer pens. Once this really posh woman of about sixty-five or more, with her expensive hairdo, had her little stash of coke, another one had a card signed by Chirac, mayor of Paris, another had a live kitten.

Apart from this the strokes we pull are truly pathetic, scrapings from the bottom of the barrel. I'm not one of those people, for example, who pinch small change from kids at the gates of primary schools, that really makes me want to puke, same with the old folk who can't walk, but some do it, they'll even use force. Basically it's a matter of being able to eat: you forget everything when you're desperate – you don't know much to start with – humanity just doesn't come into it. I want that and I want it now, otherwise I'm finished, or I finish you. Hunger makes you depressed and gives you the shakes, you mourn for your race and chuck friendship and love on the scrapheap.

Mouloud knew this woman who was starving, she even nicked the food her kids brought in their pockets from the canteen to eat and they were crying all night.

At times we're so pathetic it really gets you down. A neighbouring gang on the Oak Tree, on the same estate, last year around August/September decided to nick the statues from Vaillant-Couturier Square. They planned it like a major operation. They found a ramshackle old truck, crowbars, a winch, cables and God knows what else, they toiled away, five or six of them, all Friday and Saturday night, sweating buckets, hands bleeding. They'd heard American collectors dreamed of that sort of thing. In the end they weren't even proper sculptures, just run of the mill things made out of reinforced concrete from the fifties, worth not more than two hundred francs.

Even the statues are made out of concrete now, even the ping-pong table that's got all pitted so you can't play on it any more. A teacher once said that concrete is dead matter, plastic as well. There's no life going on inside. We are born from that and out of that, our hearts made of concrete.

This story about the statues that weren't statues makes me feel depressed and angry. You can't afford to be stupid round here, otherwise you're finished. And they often are stupid, stupid enough to swallow suppositories, stupid enough to dream that there's money arriving on the next bus – you're banging your head against the trees who don't give a damn. That's also why I go away and write this, I write slowly just to be somewhere else at that particular moment, to escape on my own, even if I can't help joining in sometimes. The others have a wall in front of their eyes, they can't see anything else, this is the life that's been waiting for them, nothing but petty crime, stuff that no one would bother with. Sometimes they get a kick out of it of course, they get shot in the arse or they get arrested, they find themselves banged up for three or four weeks, where all the guys exchange their tricks of the trade – wait till you hear what I did – when they get out they do the same old shit.

Lives in pieces, thrown all over the place, chaos and misery.

In other places you see people who go on the stage – they've found some money-spinner – or else play music, always rap of course. That rhythm is starting to do my head in, it's just the same phrase repeated over and over. Once is OK but twice is once too often. By trying to express themselves, as they say, they're all trying to outdo each other, tatatata, fucking hell, what a pain. Others make clothes, they have fashion shows, the lot – that bunch from La Courneuve had a slot on the telly. So there are some who manage to raise themselves out of the shit, who don't skulk under cover to stay out of the rain. Or else sport, but for sport you need to be gifted and work hard as well.

When you ask people, all they dream about, the blacks in particular, is becoming Michael Jordan and earning pots of money, but they haven't got what it takes. They can reach out for the basket with their little arms but the glory is way out of reach. The grimmest thing is the gym where they do combat sports, especially boxing, which stinks of filth and dried sweat, even the ring has holes in it, and kids as young as seven get their faces pummelled and their noses flattened, they go home with eyes like aubergines, only to realise six years later that they're no good and the punches you take on the skull stay with you the rest of your life.

Most of them, at least the useless timewasters around me, the association of failures and headcases, are always thinking about crime, one crime after another, a life of crime, you got a nice little number, I've got a nice little number, and then they slag off the police, shits in uniform, they're always to blame for everything. I don't rate them that highly myself, they've chased me two or three times and once they knocked me out cold with their flexible baton, the long black all-over-body one. The next day I was interviewed on telly for the one o'clock news – so tell us what happened – I couldn't believe I was on telly – what did you do to receive this beating? I told them what happened up to the point where I lost consciousness, or just about, and so I ended up on the news.

I said I didn't rate them that highly, there are some bad ones who pinch sandwiches from bars without paying for them – who are you going to complain to? You keep your mouth shut. But all the same, saying that they're the cause of all the shit is a bit over the top. Once in Shady Nook a boy was killed, he ran across the road and a police car knocked him down – all right, I can understand the anger there, I was out there chucking stones and maybe gobbing at them, but it's not often we have nights where it boils over like that. The journalists start yelling that the suburbs are in flames. It's true the place is lit up on nights like that, but afterwards they talk about it endlessly for months and it gets blown up into some terrible great world war and stuff.

But I just don't believe that. You burn a bus, four cars and smash in a dozen windows, it's not the war you think it is. You burn the things you lust after but can't have. You can never have them, so you burn them, they're there within your reach but you can't touch: big difference. But if you think when you torch them you're setting France on fire you're like a mosquito declaring war on the elephant, only if the big thing with the trunk doesn't have a telly, he's not even aware of what's going on.

What is for sure, and I agree with this, is that the cops just don't give a damn, and quite a few of them live in the neighbourhood. They always clamp down on things that don't matter: a small demo to have the basketball nets fixed and they steam in with CS gas, I'm not exaggerating, while you see drug-dealers all over the place like rabbits outside the hunting season, and guns are bought and sold without any problem, real guns, I swear you can find a Kalashnikov in good nick anywhere within a three hundred metre radius.

Our existence comes to a stop in the morning and then repeats itself the next day. It's not a state of war, of red alert, it's a long waiting for nothing, you grow old each day for nothing.

I don't see it at all as a civil war on a slow fuse. Even those well-intentioned people who come to take up our case every now and then – I don't mean official ministers, with them it's twenty minutes a year, a lot of smiling, flashing lights and a pack of journalists up their arse who stop them seeing anything in any case, and besides, if nothing ever happens, what are you going to see anyway. No, I mean those good-hearted people, the genuine ones who care for their neighbour. You have to admit they do exist, they come to resuscitate community activity – that's the trendy phrase for it, which sounds to me like the time they resuscitated my mother at the hospital when I thought she was dead, even they, and they sometimes have grants from somewhere or other, some dough to splash out on us, even they, after a couple of weeks of getting us to cut up bits of paper or perform Molière in Arabic, a language which no one speaks any more round here except the old folk, like Kabyle and others, or at the Koran school where nobody understands a thing, they think about everything except praying, and you never see anyone recruiting for the GIA, so-called, to plant bombs in the underground at Oak Tree, it's another world. I've lost the thread, I was talking about these people with their grants, they all say it's oh so complicated, such a mess, the problem has to be treated at its root – root of what you never know. That's how it is, they say, they shouldn't have made the world like that.

That's how my life looks. Perhaps I should have started by dying.

Luckily I've got my dining room in the ruins, I wonder every day how much longer I'll be able to have it, Those moments when I scratch my pen over the pages of the notebook and when I cross out and start again – I make a clean copy in the end but I'm never happy with anything – it still warms my soul, if I have one, I really feel it, at least I'm doing something, and it's all mine, even if it's total shit, which is quite possible after all. But in any case it's never out of my mind, I say words to myself as I'm walking, I'm thinking about nothing else even while I'm watching telly, or doing the shopping for my mother, or taking my sister to school or bringing her back, and then at night especially when I go to bed in my little corner – I've just got a mattress on the floor – I see words and phrases in the dark, they explode around me like shooting stars. I tell myself I should remember that one, I should engrave it deep inside, then I go to sleep and forget it, and when I wake up at three in the morning what I find strikes me as basically weak and stupid, and it's my fault for falling asleep.

Obviously my problem is also that I don't stick to the point, I lose my way.

I'm now coming back to Lila. She asked me to find a camera and I said yes more or less.

She slides her feet on the grass, she pulls her knees up and her dress falls down her thighs, my eyes follow the movement, magnetised, and of course I see her slit all closed up underneath, she gives me her casual look and says as if she was talking about the nice weather:

'If you're a good boy I'll give you a blow-job one day. Would you like to come in my mouth, Chimo?'

Luckily my dark skin stops me blushing, but I feel

embarrassed inside. I make the effort to overcome it, then I say:

'Why do you always talk about things like that?'

'What else is there?' she says.

I don't know what to suggest, I can't think of anything.

Then like a gymnast she swings her legs back, showing me everything again, then she springs forward and lands on her white feet, her dress flies up – I think there's a type of dive called the angel leap – and she heads off towards her block, lightly, lightly, a quick bye and she's off.

I stay where I am. That's all for now.

I 'll say something about yesterday, when it rained. The whole gang was down the Campana, like Ruben's father says: keep your eye on the rain, you never know when it's pretending.

Ways of feeling useless: hanging out and watching the rain.

Samy the waiter lets us get away with ordering three cokes between six of us and making them last for two hours, so there we are around the pinball machine, but there are no free games today. So we pretend to play without balls, at least it's easy to win, like when you go motorbike-riding on a chair, less chance of crashing. Kids' games, basically.

They start talking about Lila, casually, like they're not talking about her all the time.

'It doesn't make sense,' says Big Jo, 'she's bought herself a bike, she must have some cash from somewhere.'

'She gets it from her aunt's pension,' says Little Maurice.

'But her aunt owes loads of people money,' reckons Mouloud. 'They refuse to serve her half the time.'

'So she gets it from selling her arse,' says Jo.

'Have you noticed it's a man's bike?' says Ruben.

'So what?'

'Could be she does a trade. Her cunt for this or that – it happens.'

'Or else she stole her bike.'

I'm not too sure who's speaking now – they're all talking at once, with moments of heavy silence, just the sound of the pinball flippers without balls, then a couple of words here, a couple there, unfinished sentences, I never know how to write them down. Then they start again about Lila, which at least shows that they've got her on their minds.

'Apparently this big grey car came to pick her up the other night. She waited for it at the kerb, they opened the door as they drove past, she got in and off she went.'

'Did you see it?'

'Samy saw it.'

Samy signals from the counter that he didn't see anything, or else he doesn't want to admit it. But the others are getting excited, all right, it wasn't Samy that saw it, it was somebody else, nice car it was, a Mercedes or an Audi, something like that, with a telly switched on in the back.

'Where was she going to in this car?'

'She was off to sell herself, what do you think? She's growing into a right little whore, that's what I say.'

'And the more manure there is, the better it grows.'

'But if she's selling herself to guys with money,' says Little Maurice, who's the least stupid, 'she'd have enough to buy herself something better than a bike! She'd get herself a Twingo at least!'

'Maybe she doesn't dare.'

'Doesn't dare what? Why wouldn't she dare?'

'Because round here it'd be seen as a wind-up. She's not going to come back with a car! She'd have her tyres punctured the first night!'

'You're right, it'd be like she was pissing on us.'

'And her aunt would ask questions, I mean, think about it.'

'For all we know her aunt could be pimping for her. Old tarts like her get shagged out, they like to get others on the game, that's the way it works.'

Young fools talking about life like they know something about it.

'Only, if she was doing it big time,' says Little Maurice, still in dreamland, 'she wouldn't get herself a Twingo, she'd get a fleet of taxis. Come on, she'd use them as a way out of here.'

'They take her off to orgies,' says Mouloud, still off on his flight of fancy – if he sees a dress hanging up to dry in a window he goes red in the face, 'they slip off into the woods or to a furnished flat in Paris and screw her five or six at a time. Or maybe in the car without getting out.'

'They draw black curtains across all the windows.'

'They put music on or a porn video to create the right atmosphere.'

'They do six or seven circuits of the ring road in a row. They take turns to have her on the back seat, she has one up her and she's sucking another at the same time to get it ready. If you're careful you can replace the guy at the wheel without stopping the car so he can have a go as well.'

That's Mouloud talking, he's mental.

'And when they've had enough they bring her back here and slip her some cash.'

'Bye now, let's fuck again soon.'

I keep quiet, I listen to them, they're dreaming on their feet, I think it's better not to say anything, they'd only take the piss. Anyway what could I say? They might even be right. She tells me more or less the same things, more complicated things, that she fucks around as much as she can, uses mirrors, I don't know what I could say, I feel lost, all right, I feel crushed, so I lower my head in silence and watch the pinball machine without balls.

One thing's for sure, I can't tell them the things she says to me, they'd be jealous, furious first of all, then they'd call me a queer. Can't you get it up? What are you waiting for? Why don't you give her one? She's just a little whore, these blondes with light-coloured eyes are the biggest sluts, it's a well-known fact in Africa, and she proves it often enough – she comes and finds you, she says these disgusting things to you and you don't even touch her. You're like a dog who's dying of thirst and turns his nose up at a bowl of water. Are you thick or what?

I can hear these words in my head as if they were really saying them to me, I can hear them in the morning, the evening, the night as well, I dig my nails into my hands so that I don't answer myself, but deep down I tell myself yes, maybe it's true.

I remember one thing she said to me which I forgot to write down: I like talking about this with you, she said. I like your eyes when I talk to you. She likes talking about this with me.

I really don't know where to look, I don't know where the world is any more. Everything has slipped. There's my head, there are my shoulders, I'm standing on my feet, I'm resting my hands on the edge of the pinball machine. I remember this moment well, I'm not listening to the others but I can hear what they say, my heart has escaped somewhere else, I don't know where, that little muscle is not here with me.

Now and again I feel happy about our secret, that she looks at me and speaks to me, I tell myself I'm the only one, I'm the only one here she's wanked off, and I'll never forget that. At other times I'm crushed, I can feel my lips quiver and a knot of sadness in the pit of my stomach, especially those days when she's not around, maybe because she's being taken away, who knows, when I go a whole day and night and the following day without seeing her I imagine her with masked men in mirrored rooms in the Champs-Elysées, Californian-style rooms with white sunlight, orange juice and a gelatin sea in the background, and I'm quick to see the images she describes to me. I chase them away fast, as if I'm afraid of making them come true by thinking about them too hard, it's a new feeling I have all over my body, I even feel it now as I write, I can't stop talking about it and I don't know what to do about it.

Mouloud continues with his dream of fucking around the world, he's lost in his never-ending orgy in Malibu and the others listen to him like it's a song you can't get out of your head. You always know what he's going to say next, first it's sex then it's more sex, and I think about those old folk I know a bit, the really religious ones with six kids and two others dead, the father's never seen his wife naked, not ever, except perhaps a flash of shoulder – they make babies by groping in the dark and maybe praying to the Prophet for forgiveness.

What they say on telly about religion is all lies, like how the terrorists are recruiting in neighbourhoods smouldering with religious zeal. Round here at least religion's not making any headway, quite the opposite: if girls wear a yashmak it's to keep the boys at bay. One of Mouloud's older sisters once told him that in Islamic countries it's not necessarily an inconvenience for the women to be separated from the men. Round here religion's well on the way out. We still go to the mosque but it's just to pass the time, to see people you don't normally see during the week, and the Muslim centre also sometimes helps you out in small ways, they're devout guys and all, the bearded ones who fight to keep the faith alive, but for all their huff and puff there are hardly any sails left to blow into.

It's God's fault for clearing off, and the more you pray the more he clears off and stays out of sight.

The other day on the telly this white-haired Canadian said we can expect to find billions of inhabited worlds in the universe. I couldn't believe what I was hearing, yes, billions, he repeated totally serious, he thought that was a distinct possibility. So I believe God exists, I hope so, but he's otherwise engaged, engaged billions of times over.

Here's not the worst place in the world.

Billions of worlds with ghettos in flames. That makes a lot of cars and cops.

In any case no one's heard of bombers being recruited on the Oak Tree. Fanaticism is also a load of crap they drum into you to get you worked up, the same on the other estates. OK there's a lot of ducking and diving round here, the rackets, the souks, the black market and a bit of a rumble every now and again with a spot of torching if you can manage it, but that's as far as it goes. It's not like Chicago in

The Untouchables, it's not some Jihad on horseback – let's ride joyfully to our deaths, paradise awaits at the end of the ball. No one has seen the name of Allah written by a laser on the clouds. Round here it's not about conquering the world, it's just that we look for something to do and there isn't anything.

Just then in the Campana we hear this strange sound of crying. We turn round and see Samy slumped over the counter with his hands out in front of him, sobbing his eyes out. We go over and look at him, Ruben asks him what's wrong. He doesn't want to say anything at first, he shakes his head, then finally it turns out he's had the result of his test and he's HIV positive. He's known for two days and he wanted to keep it a secret but he just went to pieces. We're standing there telling him it's not serious, now they have medicines to keep you alive ten, twenty years, just look at Magic Johnson, he's still red-hot at the basket.

Of course Samy doesn't give a toss about all that, nor would I in his place, so Little Maurice suddenly remembers he's got something urgent to do with his father, something he forgot about, how stupid of me, he says, and he's out the door. The others also remember things they've got to do, Big Jo says he's been asked to take some photos at a wedding – it's a job he does every now and then – they all say bye then, Samy, don't let it get you down, see you tomorrow, the sun will come up anyway, and they scatter like farts on marble and I stay on for a while, I ask him if he wants a hand washing the glasses or something. But he gets up and says no, he wipes his eyes with a towel and doesn't look at me at all, he smiles at two guys who have just come in and serves them on auto-pilot, he knows what they do, the first is a retired gym teacher, the other is the supervisor at Mammouth who's brought his knackered moped all the way here, he's so afraid that someone will nick it.

I feel like a spare part, so I give him a wave and skip away.

Outside I'm still on my own and I walk down the street, I walk slowly since there's nothing pushing me and nothing pulling me, just trying to remember in my head what the others said and what I saw, I do that all the time so that I don't have to dig it out later when I'm writing it down and I hear her voice calling me: Chimo!

I turn round and see her on her man's bike, still

dressed like a dancer, in a skirt and a pullover and white wool socks. She brakes, she smiles like heaven opening up and says:

'I dreamed about you!'

She starts cycling round me, two or three pushes on the pedals then a bit of freewheeling, then more pedalling, I stand in the middle revolving on my feet – I'm the pole in the centre of the roundabout.

'What was your dream about?'

'Guess.'

Since I clam up she says: 'Come on, it's easy.'

I still don't say anything, because I don't dare say anything, so she laughs and, with the two of us still turning round and round, she says:

'Things you wouldn't believe. I woke up wet as a tongue. I was in a gang-bang, Chimo.'

'A what?'

'Bang is English for fuck, and a gang's a gang, see? There were a hundred of them, imagine that. I was fucking with a hundred guys at once and you know what? Chimo, they all had your face!'

She pushes harder, swings the bike right round and pedals off with her two lovely natural pistons. She calls over her shoulder:

'Have you thought about the camera?'

I don't even have time to reply. She accelerates, faster and faster, where can she be going?

I go home.

That was yesterday afternoon, I'm writing this this evening.

I'm going to tell a long story now. Afterwards I don't know what will happen.

It was yesterday, early afternoon. We were kicking a ball around on the field, like we always do after lunch, one day rice, the next day pasta, talking about nothing much as usual because nothing ever happens from Monday to Saturday, just changes in the weather and even that not every day, that's why the others and me too probably always say the same words, because what we see is always the same, and that's another way of brutalising language, and with language all the rest. It's like clothes that shrink and in the end they don't fit any more, you think you've grown too fast and you've already said your words a thousand times, listening to the others is a sort of poverty, think the same, talk the same, you might as well shut up and not think at all, it's painful to think sometimes. It's like in the morning when you have to put on your jeans, your T-shirt, your shoes, every day the same, every day the same. You see fashion shows on the telly where the guys are dressed like birds, they've even got feathers up their arses, at least they have a laugh, apparently there are girls and guys too who change their clothes three times a day or even four, and every morning I find my threads from the day before and the day before that, even though my mother uses the neighbour's washing machine in the evening every now and again.

When I put on the same clothes every morning I feel like I'm the same as the day before, that my life is not moving forward, it's like a cycle race where the race order never changes, the leaders always stay in the lead, then the pack and the stragglers, those who've picked up punctures they shouldn't have, then the antiseptic freaks, the wobblers, the ones who let themselves go, showing the whites of their eyes and slavering from the mouth, with the brush of the cleaning truck right behind them, then the crowd who watch it all go by without taking much in, you throw them caps made by sad little Asian girls, that calms their worries a little, they park their bums on the grass slope and eat their sandwiches, they have a good natter while the pack goes by, the sound of the gears is like crickets hopping, then they shake the ants out of their pants, who think they've found a new metro, they gather up their rugs but leave their rubbish, and buggered if they can remember where they parked the sodding car.

I say this because once when I was thirteen they took us in a municipal coach to see the Tour de France. It lasts a minute, zip zip and they're gone. Since then I've watched it on the telly, at least it lasts a bit longer, I really like it, especially the hard bits in the mountains, and when it's finished I look forward to next year's Tour de France, but apart from that I don't look forward to anything.

I don't look forward to anything, anything at all. I know it'll pass me by, I think I've known that for a long time. Round here you can't make any plans, it's as if someone's told you it's forbidden.

It'll all pass me by, inevitably. The others know that too deep down but they act as if they don't. They see themselves rolling in money, fighting off the chicks, any day now. Not me, I don't even care. Apart from Lila there's nothing I want. Apart from Lila there's nothing.

But as for living with her, I know I'm in cloud cuckoo land. I'm singing a song without words and without music. I tell myself every day and I write it down, but every day it starts again, Lila gets inside my head, I never manage to clear my mind of everything.

The others have cemeteries in their heads, their brains are full of graves and ghosts sitting silently on the tombstones, it's always dark in there and the fog is damp and cold. I don't manage to switch off, maybe I'm wrong and I'm making things complicated for myself. Three or four times a week I find myself in my office in the ruins and I write. It's not the best way to forget, but if they took it away from me I'd throw myself under a train – or maybe I wouldn't.

Anyway, I was saying, yesterday afternoon, that at least was out of the ordinary, her aunt comes bursting out of the block dressed like something out of a pantomime, made-up to the eyeballs, holding a wooden cross in her right hand. She rushes towards us in spite of her weight, and at first we can't make out what she's yattering on about, her voice is so high-pitched she's almost shrieking, but we make out that something nasty has happened to her little angel.

'A priest!' Aunty cries. 'A priest a priest quickly!'

I don't think I've ever seen a priest around these parts, unless they camouflage themselves concrete-colour. Having said that, I don't especially look out

110

for them, or the imams. God isn't concerned about us, or us about him.

We stand there with the ball at our feet, on our guard, we see her coming in her riot of colours. Little Maurice wonders what's brought her out, since she's never shown herself in daylight, except by mistake or to scream out the window, for maybe five years.

She's screaming like this: 'The demon, the demon!'

'What demon?' says Little Maurice.

'The demon, up there!'

'Where?'

'Up there! Up there! The demon up there!'

She's got her arms up like TV aerials, pointing her shaking sausage of a finger at the block – her rings are so embedded the flesh folds over them – you can tell she's been running, she's breathing like an animal trying to speak, but where's her heart under all that fat?

'What demon up there?' Little Maurice repeats – he often speaks for the group, that's how it is, the little ones always speak more than the big ones.

She holds her wooden cross up to the building, then she presses it to her forehead, she can't get a word out so she tries to gesture, she points to her two huge flabby breasts which tend to flop together so she has to keep pulling them apart so often. We look at her, trying to understand. She mimes two horns, she opens her mouth, she sticks out her long tongue, she even touches the laurel leaf on her cross with the tip and makes a lewd moaning sound – the tip of her tongue is all yellow as if she's been eating too much saffron – then she points to her eyes which are streaked red, and we just stand there watching this apparition in silence. It's hard to know what she's trying to say with all this arm-waving.

'I don't get it,' says Little Maurice.

And Big Jo, whose manners aren't the nicest, asks: 'So what sort of insect stung you up the arse then?'

She hears this, she closes her eyes and signals no with her hand three times: no no no not an insect. I'm not talking about an insect. Her breathing calms down a bit, the whole upper part of her bulk rises and falls, especially falls, with the sound of grating plastic underneath. No no no not an insect. She taps her head with her hand, I'm not mad she seems to be saying, no, anything but mad.

'So what is it then, Aunty?' says Little Maurice, like he hasn't got all day.

Ali and his brother don't move an inch. Bakary slowly takes two steps back, like he's got his eye on a big snake, like he's already a bit spooked at least.

'The demon up there,' she says, holding up her cross.

Bakary takes another step back, he doesn't like this at all.

Then she says between panting for breath:

'You've got to help me, children, you've got to help me. Lila and me we saw the demon. We saw it we saw it. Lila's still up there, she can't move, she's paralysed. But me ... down like a shot, like a shot. I need a priest, do you understand? You've got to help me find a reverend father. Quickly, children!'

'Like we've got nothing else to do!' says Little Maurice, not best pleased at being called a child.

'And what have you got to do, eh? Tell me that, you flaming eejits!'

That's how she talks, the aunt: she says flaming eejits and lazy good-for-nothings. It's how her type talk. She also calls us heathens and ill-bred louts, and she's right on both counts. And when she's in the mood, like that time at the window, she calls us infidels, time-wasters, flash wogs and then murderers of baby Jesus. That's not true, Ali told her, it's the Jews who killed baby Jesus not the Arabs. But the aunt explodes like a jet of water, she yells that the

Jews and the Arabs are all the same, that we are all guilty of his death just by existing, in fact, why, we kill him every minute of every day, so the Devil can now get all the way up the stairs with no one to stand in his way. Where will it all lead?

We haven't a clue where it will all lead, we're having a good laugh at her.

Because she's wailing and wringing her fat hands so much, and calling us barbarians and dogs, Big Jo quickly says that he will help her find a priest, he thinks he might know of one in a nearby parish. He's an old priest, but that doesn't necessarily mean he's useless.

'Does he know exorcisms?' the aunt demands.

None of us has ever heard this word before, I had to look it up in a dictionary in a shop to find out how to spell it. But Big Jo turns to Little Maurice and Little Maurice isn't fazed by this, he says:

'He knows them all.'

'Let's go then!' the aunt cries. 'What are we waiting for, in the name of Saint Michael!'

So off we all go to fetch the old priest in the nearby parish, all of us except Bakary, who doesn't want to come, he stays to guard the ball.

Aunty takes the lead and ploughs through the air,

waving her cross. In all her colours she looks like a walking merry-go-round, precariously balanced on two well-filled black boots, the toes about to come through. She obviously doesn't wear them very often, they won't last the day at this rate.

When we reach the Campana, where Samy the waiter, who is wearing dark glasses, is wiping the white plastic chairs on the terrace, those chairs you see everywhere, and watching Aunty and her gang go past with his mouth open, like a fish watching sinking apples, I slip off to one side behind a tree without the aunt noticing and head off back to the block.

I run up the stairs, the same defaced, dirty, worn-out cement stairs as everywhere. Even the graffiti is the same as everywhere. You open your so-called gob to talk and you say the same as everyone, so you might as well shut it. If you have to speak you should say something original. I tell myself this as I go up because I'm so ashamed to live in the middle of all this stupidity. I arrive and find the front door half open, I open it carefully since I don't know the place and if there is a demon he could be waiting for me behind the door with his fork.

I go in, Lila is there, sitting all alone on a chair in

115

the living room, her hands on her knees, which are bare, and when I come in she turns her radiant head towards me with her cathedral smile and her eyes which see all of me, and she says:

'I knew you'd come.'

'Hi,' I say, 'how are you?'

'Hi, Chimo. You're out of breath, you've been running upstairs.'

I ask her why her aunt came out like there was an air-raid on.

'Because of me,' she says.

I can already feel my flyaway soul returning, like always when she looks at me and speaks to me, my legs go from under me like I've just stepped into a swamp. It's a living room like any other, except that it's painted in gaudy colours, and Aunty has put paper flowers into the cracks in the walls and stuck golden studs on the furniture; she's made a tower-block chapel out of her flat, with a Christ who has *really* risen, according to a propaganda poster she picked up somewhere – Christ has risen, but the poster is dead – and a large red and yellow image of the Archangel Michael recommending a powder for bugs and lice on a thirty-year-old advert from Martinique – the exterminated insects lying with their legs in the air, about to be roasted in hell.

I say: 'What's this demon, then?'

'It's me,' she says.

As if I didn't know.

'What happened?' I ask.

'I told her,' she replies.

'You told her what?'

'Do you want to know?'

I'm not sure I really do want to know, I'll live to regret it, but on the other hand I don't think I could live from day to day without knowing.

So she tells me:

'This morning she started bathing me like a baby as usual, drying me and patting me all over like she does, singing hymns or whatever, then she sits me down in the armchair there and squats down in front of me with a towel for my feet, then off she goes again, hands joined in prayer before my pussy, oh it's the fruit of the promised land and the bread of angels.

'This is really starting to get on my nerves, so I tell her I've seen the Devil. I said: "Aunty, I've seen the Devil."

'First she stops her litany, her jaw drops and stays dropped, she's not breathing in, her eyes see me and don't see me, I'm afraid she's going to fall flat on her face like an old carpet, that she's going to keel over in front of me, I'm thinking what am I going to do, how am I going to move this dead weight, but she finally takes a breath and says:

‘ "You saw what?"

‘ "I saw the Devil."

‘ "You're lying."

‘ "I'm not."

‘ "How do you know it was the Devil?"

‘ "He told me." ’

From here on it's me, Chimo, writing this, but it's Lila who's telling the story. I'm telling what she told me, I'm not sure how to do it, but too bad. I'll try.

Lila continues about her aunt:

‘She starts biting her fingers above the rings, she does it all the time, you can't tell if it's to hurt herself or to stop herself saying something stupid.

‘Then she says:

‘ "That doesn't prove anything."

‘ "Why, Aunty?"

‘ "Because anyone can say they're the Devil when they're not."

‘ "It wasn't just what he said."

‘ "What then?"

' "He took his cock out, it was red and it smoked."

'Now I reckon I've gone too far, I'm expecting big trouble, but Aunty prefers to try reasoning with me. Don't be surprised, she's often like that, you think she's lost in her prayers, all her fat's wobbling in ecstasy, then she suddenly says: "Button up your cardigan."

' "The fact it's red doesn't prove anything," she says.

' "And that it's smoking?"

'Naturally, she has to think about that one. I can see her trawling through her memories. So she starts tapping her breasts with her fingertips – a sure sign she's travelling back through time. I've never known how many cocks my aunt has seen in her time, she's ultra-secretive about it, but my mother once said if they were light bulbs they would light up the Place Monge for the fourteenth of July. She was at it all the time at one stage, my mother said (Lila's mother, not mine), so she can now play the Blessed Virgin.

'But she has to think back to remember if she saw any that smoked.

' "How did it smoke?" she says.

' "A lot. Red smoke that smelled of sulphur. I had to open the window afterwards."

' "It was probably some dirty boy wearing some gadget."

' "But he wouldn't have had all that hair. Or those yellow eyes or that big rat's tail behind him."

' "A rat's tail?"

' "A huge one, it trailed along the ground."

' "How did he get in?"

' "I didn't see him come in. I hadn't got to sleep when I smelled this stink like at the abattoir, I went there once, and I turned round and there he was."

' "Where was he? Where?"

' "In my bedroom, Aunty, you know."

'She raises her voice now and asks:

' "But why in the Lord's name would he come here? What have we done to him? Have you done something?"

' "I haven't done anything," I say.

' "Did you call him?"

' "No way."

' "It's already hell around here. Why would the Devil come? What would he be looking for? What would he want to do?"

' "To bugger an angel," I say.

'Now my aunt is really horror-struck.

'She collapses to the ground shaking and saying "No no," she's kicking her legs up and I'm having a bloody good laugh to myself, and you know me, I'm not a wicked girl.

'I get out of my chair stark naked and lie down next to her, I stroke her gently and I put on my quiet voice and say:

' "And you know what, Aunty, he was naked. No one from the estate would have come round with nothing on. At least, not without warning. Do you know what he said to me when he saw that I could see him? He said: "I've come to make you mine. Because you are an angel like me, Lila."

'My aunt's lying on the carpet going "Oh-oh-oh." Just like she's trying to say Saint Michael and choking on it.

' "He waved a hand, Aunty, and whoosh, my nightie was gone, I swear. I was like I am now. He asked me to look him in the eyes, then he said: 'I'm going to give you an order, Lila. You can still say no now and I promise I'll leave. If you say no I swear to Satan you'll never see me again. But if you listen to my order, if you don't say no straight away within three seconds, then you must obey immediately without argument, without a word. Otherwise, beware.' "

' "Oh-oh," my aunt says. "Oh-oh."

'And I say: "He was holding his cock in one hand as if it was too heavy. 'All right,' I said. You wouldn't believe how wet I was getting. 'You understand, no argument, you don't ask questions and you obey straight away,' he said. I say, 'All right, but make it quick.' "

' "Oh blessed Saint Michael," my aunt says in a low voice.

' "But you know what, Aunty, he's not in any hurry, you could tell he had lots of time, if you see what I mean. He moved a little bit, he waited, I was melting, I couldn't take any more of this, with that dirty animal smell as well, then he fixed his yellow gaze between my eyes and said: 'Show me your arsehole, Lila.' "

' "Oh my God," my aunt says, tapping her feet, "Oh my God, my God."

' "So of course I did what he wanted, Aunty. Without hesitating. I turned my back to him, I knelt down on the bed and I showed him my arsehole like he wanted. I even pulled my buttocks apart with my hands so that he could get a good look. We both stayed like that in silence for at least a minute, maybe two – there are moments when you lose all track of time, you know. I couldn't even hear him breathing, maybe a demon doesn't breathe, or he breathes differently, since he lives among flames and there's no oxygen at all."

'I stroked my aunt gently, I love her deep down,

you know, she's only got me, I even stroked her a bit between her legs, but there's no room to get your hand in, and then I murmured right into her ear, like we were two women sharing a secret:

'"Afterwards he spoke to me and he said: 'You're going to turn round now, my dirty little angel, and you're going to suck my cock.'"

'Just a whisper in her ear. Aunty gave a long shudder, but not a word passed her lips.

'So I carried on, still whispering softly, very gently, to give her pleasure, you know:

'"I turned round like he wanted, still kneeling on the bed, I placed myself in front of him and he brought it towards me, still holding it in his hand, it was still smoking, with his other hand he grabbed hold of my hair – I love that, Aunty, I've always loved that, why's that do you think, maybe you do too – then he told me to close my eyes and open my mouth. I obey, that's all I want, I'm in the dark now. I open my mouth as wide as I can and I feel that warm thing which is neither bone or flesh, which is full of veins and tendons, hard soft round, which moves, which tastes like nothing else, there's nothing to compare it to, especially since it's come up from so deep in the earth. You can feel it full of warm liquid at its base, erect for you just for you, pumped full of blood, first you lick underneath it with your tongue the way you should, as you know, Aunty, and you start sucking, the world stops still days nights wars seasons, you suck, he holds your hair as if his life depended on it, you don't open your eyes, you strictly obey, you suck, you've got nothing else to do but suck, you're not really sure who you are any more or what your name is, it's something stronger than you, it's something that possesses you and to think it comes from hell as well, I try to hold it in one hand to stroke it at the same time but it's so big, I only manage to hold it with two fingers like that, see, I've gone away somewhere, where I don't know, I can't think any more, I move my fingers up and down a bit like that, giving a little squeeze as well, I do it the best I can, I've gone away somewhere I don't know where, as if I was flying blind or falling down a well full of warm water, I'm not even choking I'm sucking I'm sucking without opening my eyes and I can hear the air coming out of his mouth, the odd sigh like a man, oh, Aunty, I'm so happy." '

Like I always do with Lila I'm trying to remember the exact words she said, but I'm sure there are loads of things I've forgotten. When she was speaking Lila closed her eyes too, her head bobbed back and forward like a bunch of yellow flowers in the wind, she was gone, she looked like she was really sucking the Devil's cock, who'd come just for her.

Then she says (having stopped for two or three minutes, as if to relive her sucking binge) she says:

'My aunt's sighing too but I think it's out of distress. Or else it's because the surprise has been too much for her, but at least she's listening to me, that's the main thing, she's still in the land of the living. The fat lump is alive and kicking.'

Lila says:

'She doesn't want to listen to me, but she's listening to me anyway. She's coming slowly to the surface, now she believes me, now she doesn't, she lights up, she trembles, obviously I can't take her memories away from her but it's almost as if she's sucking along with me. Hopefully it's doing her some good at her age. She's going "Ah . . . ah . . ." quietly now, like down in her throat.

'It's the first time I've talked to her about sex openly like a grown-up. They say you don't notice babies growing up when you see them every day. I bet she thinks I'm still a virgin, you know what I mean? But I'm no Joan of Arc, my voices don't come from heaven and they preach love not war. And I'm enjoying shaking her up like that just with words. She's joining in, she finds it entertaining.

'So I carry on, just for her:

' "I hear him sigh, Aunty, then groan, almost cry the way men do, I don't know what he's getting at, if he wants me to go all the way and bring him off, but he lets go of my hair, he puts his hand on my forehead and says quickly, like he's dying for it, I swear, he says impatiently:

' " 'Turn round, I'm going to bugger you.' "

' "Oh, blessed Saint Michael!" my aunt goes, clapping her hands and drumming her feet on the ground again.

' "That's what he came for, Aunty, he came to bugger an angel. An angel can be male or female, but either way you can bugger it. That's for sure. So he takes his cock out of my mouth, it was a long one, it never seemed to end, I ask him if I can open my eyes, he says no, but I'd love to have seen it before he put it in, see what state it was in, but I don't cheat, I sense that you can't cheat with him, I don't look at anything, I turn round on my knees and put myself in the same position as before right on the edge of

126

the bed, I grab my pillow to hold on to and bite if I need to, I spread my knees slightly to get myself at the right height, and he puts it in."

'My aunt goes "Oh-oh," again and tries to take her rings off, which is impossible, but it shows how worked up she is, "Oh-oh, my God, my God," and then a jumble of confused words.

' "He doesn't put it in straight away," I say, "even though I know he's dying for it. First of all he moves it down my crack, then up again, like a blind man finding his way, then he touches my buttocks, my cunt underneath, he goes back up to my arsehole which I'm showing him and then he sticks it in. I don't know how it fits in my arse, Aunty. I've never known one as big as that. Maybe it's the heat that's loosened it up, or the situation. He pushes in and everything opens in front of it, what a feeling, Aunty, like when they tortured saints in the olden days and they saw heaven open before them, he shoves it into me, then steps back a bit to shove it in even deeper. My room smells like the zoo, I can feel him looking at me with his yellow eyes, it hurts and I don't know how to describe it, it's like this cock is lifting me from earth without pity, do you understand, without a shred of pity, just to make me understand what I am, and his contempt for my pussy that you love so much. But that's not what interests him, that much is obvious, he pushes and rams his cock in all the way, until he can't get it in any further, I'm crying out quietly from pain and not from pain, he's placed his hairy hands on my hips, he's holding me tight and he starts moving me backwards and forwards without a word, he's giving me a damn good buggering, I can feel what he's doing in every millimetre, it's almost sending me to sleep, it's something that goes beyond everything, that goes further than any other feeling and it's purely physical, I'm moving along his cock, even my soul's moving, but I wonder what he's looking for in my arsehole, what does he want, why's he doing this, how does he know that it makes me afraid but gives me the desire too, to cry out, about who knows what. I'm his, I'm ready to take whatever he gives me, yes everything, it's not even to humiliate me, it's just to put me in my place, he's not being wicked, I hope it's giving him pleasure too, that it's warming his balls, that I'll feel him come and hear him cry out." '

I'm listening to Lila talking with my mouth open, I'm not even taking in what she's saying right now, I'm just recording it. Like I said, I record everything

– it's a whole lot easier later when I'm writing, it's like I rewind the tape and I only need to copy it out. If I want to write on my own then it's really tough, I get annoyed, it doesn't come, I rack my brains, but if I make her talk it comes of its own accord, easy, easy, no question. I sometimes regret that I didn't do courses or go to hear experts give lectures, because I've got the best memory of all of them round here, even at school I was best at learning poems, I read them once and I knew them, I could recite them without making a mistake, although I sometimes got it wrong deliberately in front of the others, pretended I hadn't learned it so as not to look like teacher's pet.

It was definitely Lila who made me write in the end, though I don't know who I'll show all this to. I've never been in a bookshop; maybe what she says is so disgusting no one will read it, I've no idea, but I have heard that these days all sorts of filth gets published, that since you can't dip your wick all over the place any more because of the virus there's sex everywhere – porn films, some of them hard-core, on the telly. My parents once saw one at their cousins' in La Plaine-Saint-Denis; they left in a rage yelling that they'd write to the mayor and that the Prophet would come back with a Kalashnikov to drive out the corruption. That was before my father went off with a whore from Aubervilliers – I keep on losing my thread, I can't remember how I got started on this, I'd better go back to the beginning – yes, it was Lila who made me write, but without realising it. I'll never dare show her this, assuming I ever dare show it to anyone.

It's funny all the same, my memory, that I can remember what she says word for word or almost and I can even see her face at the same time.

She was talking about feeling him come, the sort of thing she always used to tell me she told her aunt as she lay there half-dead on their cut-price living-room carpet.

' "It was at that moment, Aunty, that I knew for certain it was the Devil. Do you want to know how I knew? Do you want to know?"

'She didn't answer directly, her throat was tight with emotion, but her chin nodded up and down, yes yes she wanted to know, oh yes her chin wanted to know.

'So, even more quietly, and taking my time, I said:

' "It was because all of a sudden – remember I had my eyes closed – all of a sudden I catch the smell of a cock in front of me, do you understand, Aunty, in front of me not behind, and then I feel the warm flesh against my mouth. What else could I do but open my lips as if I wanted to eat it? Another big cock slides slowly into my mouth, I say another, because I've still got the other one taking me from behind, and the smell of sulphur as well, the two cocks seem to be in unison, they work at the same rhythm exactly, one in front one behind, and at that moment I did something I shouldn't have – as I soon found out. Do you want to know what I did, Aunty?"

'The jelly on her chin moves up and down and I can hear a little oh-oh. Yes she wants to know what I did oh yes.

'So I say:

' "I opened my eyes."

'I stop for two or three seconds so that she's primed for what she's about to hear and I add:

' "And then I saw it was the same one. It was the same one in front of me as behind me, with his eyes like sulphur and his rat's tail flailing around all over the furniture. The same one, Aunty, I'm telling you. No one else could have come in. He had doubled himself, you see, he'd divided himself in two – you can be sure only devils know how to do that – and both cocks were red and they smoked."

'Then suddenly my aunt starts doing something I wasn't expecting, she starts rocking from right to left, from left to right, then she hurls herself and starts rolling round on the carpet like a lovesick hippopotamus – not that I've seen one but I can imagine it – she grabs the front right foot of her studded armchair, which I think is hideous by the way, she grabs this foot and somehow or other she manages to hoist herself up without help, breathing like the clappers, one knee then the other then she lifts her bum up, and then she's on her feet holding the back of the chair and she says:

' "Don't move."

'She heads with great difficulty towards the bathroom, she opens the door, and before she goes in she says:

' "Make sure you don't move. I have to go out."

'Then she locks herself in for more than half an hour. I mean, going out for her is a big event. Meanwhile I put on the clothes I'm wearing now, my leather skirt, my black pullover. When she emerges she's in Technicolor, she tells me not to move again, says she's going to save me, that I should stay close to the picture of Saint Michael if I feel afraid he might come back and she goes off like a whirlwind.'

Lila stops talking now as if to say: you know the rest.

I say:

'She was screaming that she saw it as well.'

'That's not true.'

' "Lila and me saw the demon," that's what she said.'

'Did he bugger her as well?'

'She didn't say that.'

'I tell you she didn't see it.'

'She says she did.'

'She couldn't have seen it because she was in here! It was me that told her about it. Bloody hell, Chimo, who do you believe, my aunt or me?'

'I believe you, Lila.'

She flashes me one of her sunny smiles and says:

'If you don't believe me I can't see why you're listening to me.'

'And was it true?'

'What?'

'The business with the Devil, was it true?'

'You see what you're like,' she says. 'You say you believe me then you ask me if it's true. Of course it's true. Just like I told you. I forgot to mention he had claws, do you want to see the marks?'

She turns up her leather skirt, which is quite tight to start with – she's always wanting to show me something. She's having a laugh at the same time, though. I don't know if it's better to stop her or say nothing, but at that moment there's an almighty din on the stairs and they all arrive: first the aunt with all the lads and a young priest wearing glasses and civilian clothes. He looks laid back but wary. He's not the excitable type who sees a devil lurking in every bush, and he's not the old one that Big Jo knows, but another one that they were told about, a new one. So he starts asking questions: what time was it? Where did it happen? He even asks to see the room where the alleged supernatural event took place. Then there's a bit of confusion when Lila's replies don't tally with the aunt's visions – did the aunt see the Devil or not? There's a lot of disagreement and arguing. I'm thinking this could go on for ever, a few of the others are starting to get bored and what's more Lila doesn't say anything about her fuck from hell, just that the Devil came and really frightened her. She looks across at me three or four times as if to tell me to keep shtumm, another secret between the two of us, maybe, and the aunt's

134

going frantic, she's not sure of anything any more, who knows if Lila even told her about the sex session and all that, the aunt is just raving that the Devil wanted to steal the body and soul of an angel of the earth, after that she starts saying her prayers. I realise that I've had the cherry on the cake and there's no more pudding, so I leave discreetly to go and write all this down before I forget.

And I'm just finishing it now.

This priest being the trendy modern type, I don't think he really believed this story about the Devil, though he was quite polite to the aunt when he saw she was so shook up about it all. He said that devils are few and far between these days, even with the return of religion, and that the young girl should perhaps be examined, there are cures for that sort of thing. Basically he calmed the situation down, he didn't want to get too embroiled. What he was saying was that it was the doctor's business not his, and with these smooth words he slipped away.

But the aunt had been so convincing when she spluttered out her story about the Devil with his fire and brimstone cock that the whole estate erupted. Most of the locals believe her: see, the Devil has come to the Oak Tree, you notice he didn't go anywhere else, just the Oak Tree, we've obviously got something the others haven't, and I know what it is, it's Lila. But the others aren't especially thinking about her, they see themselves as singled out, it's like they've won the Lottery, they're proud even, I mean, the Devil's not just anybody, and suddenly he's being spotted all over the place with his hoofs and horns and flying broomsticks.

I'm wondering what the Devil could have been looking for round here. If I was in his shoes I'd go to some better-off neighbourhood, the more money you have the guiltier your conscience. Round here even the car park is damp, the rain seeps in underground, we call it 'the house of toads'. The sports centre is so dilapidated that even the high bar is bent. Everything's in a terrible state. If you look at the cladding on the buildings for an hour or two you can see it crumbling. The girls all steer clear of you, except for three or four that frighten the dogs, you haven't even got enough to take them dancing; and then there are the others who are on the game, they look right past you, they can tell there's a drought in your pockets, that you don't really exist, that you hang around morning, noon and night, that even in your dreams you don't have a plan. So the Devil on top of all that, I can only see it in two ways: either he's made a mistake, we didn't need him at all, he's like rain falling on the sea – it's hell enough as is, that's what the aunt reckoned; or else it's you, big brother, you've picked a good spot, take whoever you want, we were starting to get bored without you, yes, we were missing you, honest.

All of a sudden I remember my dad, he left when I was twelve, he always used to say take care, son, they don't have fans in hell. I didn't know what he meant, but I do now. That was how he used to speak; he was always depressed, my dad, and sometimes it comes back to me. For example, he'd say: if it rained shoes I'd be a snake, or else, if I sold coffins no one would die, if it rained soup I'd only have a fork, if I inherited a supply of fog the sun would shine at night. When you asked him where he came from he'd say not from home, and I wouldn't know what he meant.

He also used to say: there are people who eat dates and there are others who get the stones.

Sometimes he comes into my head when I least expect it and yet I never hear how he's getting on, if he's had other kids with his whore or not, where it is he's unhappy now; all that's left are these things he used to say all day long, I can't even remember his face.

Another strange thing, now I think about it: you know tomorrow will be the same and yet you want to get there as soon as you can, you want time to get a fucking move on so you can get to the same thing or something worse.

I was born with nothing and I still have nothing. And tomorrow is nothing.

Why, I ask myself, is it impossible to live in peace on such a planet, why are there haves and have-nots, why do farmers pulp tonnes of tomatoes when you're hungry, why, it's all so screwed-up and complicated in this fucking world.[1]

---

[1] The final two paragraphs were written in the margin of page 50 of the second notebook without any indication of where they belong. We have placed them arbitrarily at the end of this chapter.

After two or three days the world and his wife have seen the Devil at the window, the Martinique lot in Block B said it was the zombie creature that had been tracking them from back home and had finally caught up with them. This caused that lot from the Antilles to panic – prayers, trembling, the whole shebang, they even sacrificed a cockerel. At the same time the Malians from Block C reckoned no way, it's not some voodoo zombie, the Devil came from Africa, that's the only place you see smoking cocks and that doubling-up trick is pretty common over there, it's got to be the spirit of tatamoké or bouboubadou or whatever who's strode across the desert and the sea, only he could do that, and he's going to give other girls the shafting he gave Lila, the hour has come, he'll even need helpers, for what no one knows exactly. Everyone has their own ideas except me. For some of them it's the height of excitement, for others it terrifies the balls off them.

The traditional Catholics like the aunt – an endangered minority since Christ is losing ground, some of them say he ought to get rid of the pope, he's tucked up in the cops' pocket, he gets up to all sorts – the Catholics on the estate who still believe had a procession with holy water and exorcisms, I know the word now, at least I've learned something, and a lot of 'Be gone, Satan, clear off you filthy creature', the banners they were brandishing looked like those adverts for the dairy produce of Auvergne, the one with Saint Michael was the highest of the lot. There were about twenty of them sprinkling the concrete left and right with a silver club filled with holes, the aunt leading them in all her colours, all of them singing hymns that set your teeth on edge.

The Malians taunted them with animal noises from their building, one of them even bared his bum at Saint Michael as he went past – he's one of those from the African fighters' club, he wears braid bracelets round his arms and he's always challenging everyone at the Campana, in the street, everywhere, except when there's some real fighting to do. At the last big competition at Évreux he was apparently knocked out in four seconds. But baring his bum at the holy banner was a bit provocative all the same, the Catholics bristled as they went past. I thought they were off on a mini crusade, especially as the aunt was giving us one of her black looks.

But the priest just laughed. They said he was being irreligious, I think he was really amused to see a black arse right there and then. Of course they had a go at him for smiling. He was only there because they forced him to come, apparently he hangs out with Communists – that doesn't explain everything, but like the rest, the Catholics are getting very hard-line these days, they have to if they want to keep their customers.

In the evening it started to deteriorate. The Malians lit a big fire and slit a sheep's throat, the blood poured into the ground, then around half-ten the tom-toms started, because the night's the time to put the wind up the Devil, during the day he's asleep and doesn't give a toss. So around eleven o'clock there's a swirl of dancing with feathers and the tom-toms still going strong, everywhere people shouting 'Shut up down there,' out of their windows, chucking pots of piss on them. They carry on dancing themselves into the ground. Untel calls the police who don't want to meddle in a black dance, go and dance with them, the cops say, hope the Devil buggers the lot of you up to your nostrils, that's how they speak at night, during the day they're more polite.

So the Antilles lot and a few old Catholics go down with clubs and screwdrivers and kitchen knives and they steam straight into the Malians and it's all-out war. The sheep's not the only one who'll get his throat cut tonight, I say to myself, but I keep out of the way, all this hysteria's got nothing to do with me.

It's dark up above and it's dark down below, there's fierce fighting and screams and yells all over, I can see nothing but a confusion of shadows, I can hear mainly moans and groans, a couple of cars have been set alight, good idea to leave them there, it's hell straight out of hell and in hell there are no cops, you can be sure of that at least. Everyone's going round disembowelling each other in the chaos, there's moonlight, it's really frightening, the women's screams as well.

And then it dies away, no one knows why, maybe because it's starting to smell of blood. Nearly everybody has gone after ten or fifteen minutes except for three or four who've come off worst, they're still hanging around, groaning, obviously injured, and two chickens running around beating their wings crazily, bumping into everything including the sheep, which isn't cooked yet. Chickens at this time of night should either be sleeping or dead.

Three or four dark figures are still fighting on the old lawn, the rest finally drift away. The fire for the sheep-roast is about to go out, and not a single cop has shown his arse after hours. I've been hiding in the dark. I start to head off home, skirting round the battlefield, and there's Lila, for once it's me that sees her first, flat against a tree like she's been captured by Red Indians. She's got her head on one side, she doesn't move, her eyes are fixed on the idiots who are still fighting.

I approach her in total silence, I'm looking at her now, she's slid her left hand under her skirt which is rippling slightly, even though there's no wind this evening, and I can see her other hand very clearly, gripping the bark of the tree, the veins standing out, hard enough to make her nails bleed.

The next day two young guys from the telly turned up with camera in hand and started filming the brown marks on the ground and sniffing around for information, but we didn't want to tell them anything. Big Jo actually wanted to pick a fight with them. They really are like flies buzzing around a bleeding nose; they're always making out the estates are going up in flames. We slag them off about this and call them shit-eaters. The two guys reply that it's their job, it's how they make their living, they'd heard there was a holy war going on with bloody sacrifices and someone had mentioned the Devil.

They'd also heard about this blonde girl whose rape set all this off, but they're not sure who raped her. They ask where she lives, which block at least, we don't tell them the truth, I know more than anyone but I play the idiot. Come on, do us a favour, they say, give us a clue, they insist.

I've got one eye on their camera, thinking about

my project with Lila, which I don't quite believe in by the way, but this particular camera is too complicated, I'd never work out how to use it. I know that Ruben and the others are thinking along the same lines, a nice present from French television, but the two guys are taking every precaution. All right, all right, no need to get mad, it's no big deal, no one died, no need to be like that about it, we get given a hard time too sometimes, but a whole gang starts running across from Block G, three or four of them have their hands in their pockets, the storm clouds are gathering, so the two guys get quickly back into their car and they're on their way.

Little Maurice says: 'Fucking bastards, they think it's a fucking zoo. They make you want to set the whole place on fire even if you're not in the mood.'

Then we go. Bakary and Mouloud go off to try to gatecrash a few windscreens on the Avenue Émile-Zola, but the Algerians run that racket, you have to pay for your traffic light in advance, or watch your back for the razor.

I'm amazed at the state of things sometimes.

We all throw up over this estate, it's a total disgrace, the way people chuck everything out the window, but you still cling to your bit of concrete, this bit of concrete rather than another, I don't know how to say this, you're from here, that's for sure, lots of people are born here, the world has been designed before they got here, not necessarily how they would have liked it, but they need some place, and they don't have anywhere else: their country is a tower block, concrete like everywhere else, so they don't give a toss about trees and grass.

When you leave the estate you miss it.

It's unbelievable, but it's true, I swear. You actually end up loving it.

It's unbelievable, but it's true – well, not always true, but sometimes it is. Mouloud told me that his aunt and uncle and their family at Montfermeil cried when they blew up their tower. Yet they never stop complaining about all this shit, that they shouldn't make human beings live in this fucking pig-sty, then when it's demolished they cry.

Imagine a bird in a nest made of reinforced concrete, there's no more straw on earth, so what happens to the eggs?

I honestly don't believe I'd cry if I went away from here. It could be worse, that's true for everyone, it can always be a lot worse. The idea of going off and getting lost somewhere, still without a penny to my name, there's piles of cash all over the place and I'm empty-handed, what's the point of leaving, I say to myself, it's the same shit everywhere else.

I still wouldn't cry if I had to go away, only if I had to leave Lila. She's the only reason to stay or go. Otherwise I don't know what planet I'm on, I don't know what's north and what's south, I'm here now, I could be somewhere else, I'm sure it's the same everywhere, when you're skint you're poor wherever you are, the world is invisibly divided up into different levels, you up there, me down here.

You see students who'll do anything to earn a bit of money for their studies, I don't give a damn, there's nothing I could study, and all those guys in the street with their little signs, spare some change please, I couldn't even do that. I haven't lost the right to complain, I never had it. Except that the Right say it's all our fault, the immigrants.

There's soon going to be one hell of a rumble.

The people who live here come from all over the world, except Asia, because the Chinese don't mix, and sometimes there's as much fighting as on the night of the Devil. People don't mix as well as concrete, the more you want them to be the same, the more they stay one thing or another, so in the end they rub each other up the wrong way.

Big Jo has something to do, he says, no one knows what. I think he and a mate of his have cut up a big piece of road grilling and are trying to make grills to sell.

Little Maurice and Ruben are off to hang out somewhere, they don't know where. Just before we split up Lila arrives on her bike, she sees the four of us together from the distance but she only calls to me as she goes past, she just says: 'Hi Chimo!'

It's like the others weren't there, she doesn't see them, her eyes look right through them. They're not happy about that, naturally, after all, all the fighting and the injuries are because of her, there are two in hospital with knife wounds, and she carries on all high and mighty on her man's bike.

As usual they call her a slut and a tart through clenched teeth, it's the only two words they know. At first when they saw her they were knocked out by her themselves, they gave her the glad eye and they said that's a little bit of all right, God had a good day there, he made an effort with that one, whatever it costs it's worth it, and now they do nothing but insult her.

Maybe they're afraid, I tell myself. She scares them,

and the demon too. She scares me sometimes. I'm scared of what she might make me do.

When she goes past I don't dare reply in front of the others. I just give her a little wave and she dances away.

It's already the end of October, it'll soon be winter.

Now the thing I couldn't even think about, I told myself no I'm not going to write this down, I'll never be able to do it, but I am going to write about it before I leave, because I am going to leave afterwards, I can't see what else to do.

If I ever had any hope it's all gone now, all gone, because you can't buy hope, it's not for sale, the big stores don't stock it, and you can't nick it from anyone else, you even reach the point where you can't remember the word and you wipe it from your mind. And what can I say, I don't know what, all alone in my ruins as it gets dark, I'm totally depressed and confused.

And another thing, the Devil does exist. I don't know about God, but the Devil does, he's everywhere and heaven is nowhere, just because hell exists doesn't prove there's a heaven.

I now have to say what happened, I've brought two candles along so I can have a go at least, but I

151

feel more alive already, the wind moves me easily, the rain goes through me and hits my bones. I'm talking but I'm saying nothing, I decide to go right and I go left, and it's been like this since the day before yesterday, I don't know where I am any more, I don't recognise anything any more, it's like I'm asking directions to lost things, I'm even on the wrong floor.

I found a camera, right. Samy had one and he lent it to me, it was a bit old but it worked and there was even a tape with it. All the same I was only half pleased, because I didn't know if I'd have the bottle to film her like she wanted, being fucked by two masked men, and I'm wondering what I'm getting out of all this. Do I get a sweetie or not. She spoke about giving me a blow-job one day, about bringing me off in her mouth, that's not something you forget, but I wanted more.

On the other hand my heart was putting the brakes on, it didn't need this, it needed something else and I told myself what this something else was: you'll lose her if you let her suck you off, you'll just be a fuck like the others, one more or less, you won't be any further forward in terms of feelings, what matters is that she picked you out, it's the only thing in the world that matters, she says hello to you and not to the others, she talks to you, she lifts her skirt for you, so if you take the fatal step, you join the queue of those waiting to fuck her, you're back in the pack of nobodies, you're nothing but a leaf on the tree, watching out for the autumn winds.

I was worried about this, I got up in the night to look at the camera and I asked myself: do I tell her or not? I really didn't want to be the cameraman at her orgy, I don't mind saying I felt afraid it would hurt to watch her fucking other guys, I'm not the type that likes that sort of thing, I was afraid of forgetting myself and destroying everything and losing her for ever.

At the same time I told myself: if it's not you it'll be somebody else. There's no shortage of voyeurs. And if Lila's got the idea in her head she'll do it, as sure as winter comes. Might as well be you as a stranger. You shouldn't have let her wank you off on the bike, then. But maybe I was just trying to build up my courage, I never know what I'm really thinking.

I'm describing how I was in the week before all this, I was totally confused, I was going to tell her then I wasn't, even my little sister noticed it, she asked if I was in love, or unhappy, or if I had the chance of a job somewhere. I told her no, not at all.

Now I'm here in my office, it's harder than ever to write, I've just lit a candle and stuck it on to a block of plaster, I pinched the candles from my neighbour when I took her her mail, she never uses them anyway, she's almost blind, I'm sitting here writing in the dark or almost, it's a bit cold, it seems like I'll soon be out of here, the builders are coming back and it'll soon be too late in the year to sit out here, the days are getting shorter, it was my summer office and that's it.

I'm going to write for a long time this evening, I'm not sure two candles will be enough.

I'm writing very badly, I'm not able to reread it to tidy it up. I've never written so badly.

Three days beforehand Mouloud and Ruben had told me they'd seen Lila go off in a limousine again, or more or less, the same type of car with curtains in the window, but I'm not sure I believe them, especially now. I think they were just having mad fantasies about her and they were already thinking about dragging her down.

I'm finding it really difficult to say this in the dark, I don't want to write well any more, in any case I won't write any more, if she can't speak to me any more what would I write anyway, and what would be the point.

My mother didn't see me come home, she must be thinking that I'm hanging out somewhere and she'll be cursing me under her breath.

I met Lila three hours later, she was walking really slowly down the street, scraping her shoes along the ground with both hands behind her back, I caught up with her and asked her where did you go to in that car, she said what car, she looked like she was coming down from a trip.

'My mates saw you,' I say.

'Saw me what?'

'They saw you get into a car and drive off.'

'When?'

'Just now, today.'

'Your mates are a bunch of subnormals,' she says, 'haven't you worked that out yet? Ruben can't count past twelve and he smells so bad even the ants avoid him. And Ali, have you seen his teeth? He doesn't need a dentist he needs a chimney sweep. Mouloud's got sex on the brain, for him the world's one big porn show, he's the sort of weirdo who frightens the girls, I bet he wanks off four times a day till his arm aches. And Little Maurice with his stupid prattle and his green skin, he only talks to forget how short he is, he's so far from the sky you'd think he was a limp bit of weed, the sort that makes cats throw up.'

And she carries on like this, in a rage, she does them all: Big Jo is a certified loony, he's so thick even the others have noticed, and the others are the same, white or not, they're all gutless wastes of space. I've never heard her talk like that, with real anger, I'm surprised she even knows all their names.

'They're a bunch of useless spastics, they're only half human. I don't look at them when I pass them, I'm too afraid I'll pollute my eyes, so they hate me, they spit on me, I know they do. But you can spit on the fish's head and the whole sea won't make it wet. There's nothing they can do to me. They call me a little tart, so what? Maybe I like it, eh, Chimo? Maybe I like being a little tart? I'm not for the likes of them, they know that at least, no chance of them getting that wrong. I'd have any trash on earth before I'd look at those poor shitheads, they've got too many flies buzzing round their arses, it must be lovely inside their pants. Anyway, I don't give a fuck, anything they say about me just washes over me.'

She pauses for a moment, then continues for me:

'It pains me sometimes to see you with them,

Chimo. I tell you, it really pains me, you're not on the same level. I know that too, you see. That's why I'm nice to you at least. Because I am nice to you, aren't I, you can't deny that.'

I don't disagree with her.

I'm a bit shaken up by what's happening to me now. Obviously I wasn't expecting it. All of a sudden she's talking about me personally, like she never has before. Though she is acting strange, walking slowly down the street all on her own.

She comes right up to me, she looks a bit calmer, she looks at me like no one else could. Seeing her there, I'd die for her.

'But sometimes I think you're just like the others,' she says, 'that you're no better than them. That you've got an empty life ahead of you, that you don't have a thought in your head. Like I told you, that's where blokes always fall down.'

She taps her head lightly as she says:

'That's all there is, Chimo, do you understand, that's all there is. The rest's just dust. You've either got it up there or you haven't, and I thought you did have something. What I mean is, more than the others, you see.'

It hurts me to hear this, and I don't know how to reply.

It gets worse, she says:

'And I thought you were my friend. You knew all my secrets, I told you everything, but I was wrong about you, you're just as false as everyone else, just as insignificant.'

She spins right round but she doesn't go far, she turns round again towards me and she says:

'The car? What about the car? Am I not allowed to have any friends then? Friends who'll take me out for a drive when I feel like it? Am I not allowed? And is it any of your business?'

I make a sign to say no it's none of my business.

'Just because I gave you a hand-job that makes it your business?'

'No no,' I say.

Then all at once things get confused, she says:

'What I said to you about the Devil, you knew it wasn't true, that I made it up to get my aunt a bit excited, you knew that, but you didn't say anything. Why not?'

I don't reply.

'You could have avoided all that fighting and chaos, but you didn't, you said nothing. I was just having a laugh, trying to get my aunt going, I'm fed up with all her drivel. You don't believe the Devil really exists with his big rat's tail? And if he did exist he'd bother coming here? You full of shit or what?'

I feel like saying yes, I do believe in the Devil. But she changes again and gives me her fatal smile.

'Even when I was on my own I thought about you. I once had a wank and thought about you, you don't have to believe me. I even thought we might get married, that we might have kids.'

All these words wound me like poisoned darts.

'So what if I am a little tart? What do you want me to do? Have you got a better idea? Have you ever come up with a better suggestion?'

She looks like she's about to cry.

I feel annihilated, I'm shaking, nothing like this has ever happened to me, I want to grab her and hold her tight, I think I should have done it but I couldn't, I don't know why, but I couldn't. There was something I was still afraid of.

It was too late when I realised what she was saying. I'd forgotten who I was, and to mention the camera, I'd forgotten everything. She was already hurrying away, without turning round this time, on her own, and I couldn't find anything to say, couldn't express myself at all.

It was the stupidest moment in my entire life.

*

My dad often used to say things that I didn't understand, things his dad used to say to him, like the blind man puts his own child's eyes out, or the forest burns with its own wood. This evening I'm starting to understand a little. Who knows why my dad left, who knows where he is and if he thinks about his son sometimes, and now I'm going to leave, my mother will be abandoned all over again, but I'm just a drain on her, I don't give her anything, she'll be relieved if I leave, I reckon.

What my dad said is true, I can feel it now, I'm looking at the second candle, which is still burning, a couple of insects flying round it, trying not to get burned, and so on all night long, the candle will die before they do.

I don't know where I'll go, I've got no idea, I haven't got a heart any more, I mourn for my race and all the rest.

I'm going to tell what happened in the end quickly, without getting in a muddle, I haven't got long to write.[1]

---

[1] The final three pages of the manuscript are covered in crossings-out and are very difficult to decipher.

I finally make my mind up. I pick up the camera and I go round to see her, I'm going to tell her I'll do it, I just hope she'll open the door to me.

This was yesterday afternoon. Samy calls out to me as I go past the Campana, he says my mates have been round, they had some cash because Big Jo had sold four padded jackets he'd nicked off a lorry at a red light. Samy says they were really knocking it back, they got over-excited and started talking about Lila, they were saying she'd get hers one day, the stuck-up little slut, why not right now, then they left, that was over two hours ago, no one's seen them come back.

'Where did they go?' I say.

'I don't know. To Lila's, I think.'

I don't know why, but fear grips me in the pit of my stomach, I leave and start running, I go in, I dash upstairs, I go into Lila's through the open door and I can't describe what I saw.

The aunt is lying in the corner with her hands tied, she's not moving, she's got a plastic bag over her head. Lila is tied to the settee with a rope, the settee is turned over on its side, Big Jo is holding Lila by the shoulders, they've stuffed a dishcloth in her mouth, Mouloud is fucking her, two guys from

Block G are holding her legs, she's got her head back and her eyes closed.

I go in and move towards them, they're grinning at me and a guy from Block G says, 'There, she won't be putting it about so much after this. You can join the queue if you like.' I start lashing out with the camera and swearing, I don't even know what I'm saying, Big Jo and Mouloud clear out straight away, I don't see Little Maurice, Ali and Ruben, maybe they're there but I don't see them, or Gilbert, the table's been turned over as well, the contents of the drawer have been emptied on the ground, I pick up a knife and start waving it about, they shout, 'Don't be stupid, Chimo,' they clear out one after the other, at that moment I notice the blood flowing over Lila's open thighs, I realise what that means, I take the dishcloth out of her mouth, it's almost fallen out anyway, I cut her rope, at first she says nothing, she just breathes quickly quickly, then she opens her eyes and she sees me.

She sees me with the knife in my hand right in front of her and she starts screaming, 'You too, you too', it's like she's blown a fuse, her eyes are red, 'You too, you bastard, you bastard,' her face is filled with horror, it all happens so quickly that I don't know what to say, her aunt seems to be stirring a bit but not enough to get up, at least they haven't killed her, I tell myself, no they haven't killed her, she's moving, I finish cutting the rope, I hold out my hand to help her but she recoils screaming, 'No no no,' she stubs her foot on the camera lying on the floor and staggers, that's where I made my mistake I reckon, I try to go to her to hold her hand and reassure her, I come too close, I forget I'm holding the knife, the window was open behind her, Lila topples backwards crying, 'No no, you bastard,' she falls over the rail with her arms stretched out, she falls and I don't see her any more. I lean over and she's lying five floors down in a broken heap, dead, only her hair moving a little and the blood on her thighs – that's all I can see from where I am.

I've still got a bit to say, it's not very much.

I don't know how I got down, I don't remember any stairs, I could have jumped myself, already there were people down below looking at her split head and open eyes.

They were saying hospital, poor girl, the police.

Then it all happened very quickly, I can't remember very well, the police took me aside, they said come on tell us you raped her with the others and threw her out the window, come on, but the aunt had taken her head out of the bag and said it wasn't me, and so did someone else who had been watching from the landing, I told them everything I knew about that day, the other days are my secret, they're not for the cops or anybody.

It's just for me, for me to write.

They've got no reason to hold me, the cops say, I can do what I want, I'm free. It's really good to be free, I thank them and say goodbye.

They also questioned Samy.

Three or four of the gang were arrested.

And apparently the aunt doesn't talk any more, it's the biggest thing that's ever happened to her.

I've seen death for the first time, I wasn't expecting it.

My candle will go out in four or five minutes and it will be dark and windy. I'm not going home, I've decided, I'll spend the night here and wait for the post office to open and send this off tomorrow I don't know where.

I've been a pain to everyone all my life, I should never have been born, but there it is.

Lila was the only thing, Lila and what she said, I

don't know if that makes sense, there wasn't anything else.

I won't see her again, I heard they are going to cremate her, I won't see her again and that's it.

Also published by Fourth Estate

THE KISS

Kathryn Harrison

'My father takes my face in his hands. He tips it up and kisses my closed eyes, my throat. I feel his fingers in the hair at the nape of my neck. I feel his hot breath on my eyelids.'

Kathryn Harrison's parents married at 17 but were forced apart by disapproving parents within a year, by which time their only child, Kathryn, had been born. She was not to see her father again until she was ten. Instantly, they were attracted; they even looked alike. By the time Kathryn was twenty, the two had fallen into a passionate affair. This is the searing account of the author's four-year affair with her father.

'One of the most startling books you are ever likely to read'
Observer

'Powerfully written, utterly compelling' *Mail on Sunday*

'Shocking, terrifyingly honest – and beautifully written'
Elle

£6.99 paperback   ISBN 1 85702 708 6

A VICIOUS CIRCLE

Amanda Craig

A brilliantly written satire of modern manners, dissecting and connecting modern London, from its literary circuit to its hospitals and slums, as well as giving a funny and poignant portrait of childbirth and motherhood.

This gripping, moving and hilarious novel introduces seven characters, each of whom has a profound effect on each other's lives. Each must choose between probity and self-interest in love and work. Some compromise themselves completely; others oscillate between vice and virtue. Others are redeemed by twists of fate. For in a vicious circle, nothing is certain except change.

'The greatest English novelist under the age of 50 has just stepped onto the stage' A. N. Wilson

'A corker of a novel about class divisions, friendship, motherhood, betrayal – about The Way We Live Now'
Daily Mail

£6.99 paperback   ISBN 1 85702 685 3

DIAMOND GEEZERS

Greg Williams

A London urban thriller – hilarious, disturbing, sharp as a broken bottle and brutally realistic.

In a world of polo geezers and page three princesses, terrace legend Russell Fisher gets a job as Ron Chisholm's minder. Ron's a local villain who runs a tidy loansharking and gambling operation. But Ron's got something else Russell wants, something feminine . . .

Councillor Goodge has rubber-stamped the odd late licence for Ron's clubs. Local residents are pressuring him about race crimes. He needs a bit of muscle and he knows just where to find it.

Kaffir Khan's on life support. He owes folding to Ron, so he's had a visit from Ron's little brother, Trevor. It isn't personal. It isn't even a lot of money. But Trevor's a psycho. And Trevor's hired Russell for Ron . . .

'The dialogue crackles and spits off the page like a pit bull with a hangover' *Daily Telegraph*

'Fast, violent, comic and full of gritty realism' *Esquire*

'Fast-paced, funny and frightening' *Cosmopolitan*

£6.99 paperback   ISBN 1 85702 749 3

All Fourth Estate books are available at your local bookshop or newsagent, or can be ordered direct from the publisher.

Indicate the number of copies required and quote the author and title.

Send cheque/eurocheque/postal order (Sterling only), made payable to Book Service by Post, to:

Fourth Estate Books,
Book Service By Post,
PO Box 29, Douglas
I-O-M, IM99 1BQ

Or phone: 01624 675137

Or fax: 01624 670923

Or e-mail: bookshop@enterprise.net

Alternatively pay by Access, Visa or Mastercard

Card number ☐☐☐☐☐☐☐☐☐☐☐☐☐☐☐☐☐

Expiry date ....

Signature ....

Post and packing is free in the UK. Overseas customers please allow £1.00 per book for post and packing.

Name ....
Address ....
....
....

Please allow 28 days for delivery. Please tick the box if you do not wish to receive any additional information. ☐

Prices and availability subject to change without notice.